W9-BTM-358

The Last Song

EVA WISEMAN

Tundra Books

Text copyright © 2012 by Eva Wiseman
Published in Canada by Tundra Books,
75 Sherbourne Street, Toronto, Ontario M5A 2P9

Published in the United States by Tundra Books of Northern New York,
P.O. Box 1030, Plattsburgh, New York 12901

Library of Congress Control Number: 2011923466

Library and Archives Canada Cataloguing in Publication

Wiseman, Eva [date]
The last song / Eva Wiseman.

ISBN 978-0-88776-979-5

I. Title.

PS8595.I814L38 2012   jC813.'54   C2011-901453-X

We acknowledge the financial support of the Government of Canada
through the Book Publishing Industry Development Program (BPIDP) and
that of the Government of Ontario through the Ontario Media Development
Corporation's Ontario Book Initiative. We further acknowledge the support
of the Canada Council for the Arts and the Ontario Arts Council for our
publishing program.

ONTARIO ARTS COUNCIL
CONSEIL DES ARTS DE L'ONTARIO

Printed and bound in the United States of America

This book was produced using recycled materials.

1 2 3 4 5 6   17 16 15 14 13 12

For my parents
and
my husband and children

ALSO BY EVA WISEMAN

A Place Not Home
My Canary Yellow Star
No One Must Know
Kanada
Puppet

ACKNOWLEDGMENTS

I would like to thank my husband and children for their belief in me. They are my first readers and my first critics.

I must also extend my appreciation to Maria Luz Alvarez for advice about the music of Spain in the fifteenth century.

The songs at Isabel's betrothal in Chapter 2 were composed by Juan de Anchieta and Juan de Enzina, respectively, in the fifteenth century.

My thanks are also due to my editors, Kathy Lowinger and Kelly Jones, who never led me wrong.

Finally, I would like to mention the Canada Council for the Arts, the Winnipeg Arts Council, and the Manitoba Arts Council for their generous support.

And the Children of Israel wept and said:
"Who will feed us meat? We remember the fish
that we ate in Egypt without charge, and the
cucumbers, melons, leeks, onions, and garlic.
But now, our life is parched, and there is nothing.
We have nothing to anticipate but manna."

THE HEBREW BIBLE, NUMBERS 11:4–6

Chapter 1

Toledo, Spain

FRIDAY, SEPTEMBER 23, 1491

"What do you see? Is there a handsome stranger in my future?"

The slave girl's fingers tightened around my hand, but she remained silent.

"Tell me what you see, Mara!"

The slave raised her head. Her dark eyes glimmered in her ebony face. "Nothing, mistress. Nothing at all." She dropped my hand.

"Tell Doña Isabel her future!" my friend Brianda said sharply.

Reluctantly, the girl took my hand again. Her index finger traced the center crease running down my palm. She shuddered. "Your life line is short, my lady," she stammered. "It means unhappiness and hard times in your future."

A shiver ran down my back. "Tell me more."

"Have you lost your senses, Mara?" Brianda cried. She pointed to the door. "Out with you!"

The slave girl fixed her gaze on the floor and curtsied deeply before backing out of the room.

"Unhappiness? Hard times? What can she mean?" I took a deep breath to steady my voice and shrugged to show that I didn't really care.

"Isabel, forget about the slave. She knows nothing. My mother says that all slaves are ignorant heathens."

"But they are well-versed in the black arts. Did you notice how nervous she became when she looked at my palm?"

"I don't understand why you even asked the slave about your fortune. Your papa will find you a fine cavalier to marry."

"I thought that it would be fun to have her read my palm. Papa won't be looking for a husband for me for another year, not until I turn fifteen. He always says that he and Mama can't bear the idea of losing me yet. He promised to choose someone I like."

"Oh, I wish that I wasn't younger than you! I want my father to find somebody for me too."

"He will. Be patient. You're only thirteen." I grabbed her arm and pulled her toward the shrine of the Virgin Mary in a corner of her bedroom. I, too, had one at home. "Let's pray to the Virgin for our happiness."

"Look how beautifully I decorated the altar in the Virgin's honor."

Two tall vases blooming with white roses sat on either side of the Virgin's portrait, which hung on the wall. The holy mother was gazing with love at the Christ child in her arms. I crossed myself and sank to my knees. So did Brianda.

I closed my eyes and began to pray. I prayed for health and for happiness. I felt at peace – as I always did when I addressed our savior's mother.

The door to Brianda's room swung open and my slave Sofia appeared. "Doña Isabel, it's getting late. We must return home," she said. "Your lady mother will be angry if we aren't back before the setting of the sun."

My cloak covering me from head to toe, I followed Sofia as she used her elbows to cut a path through the throng clogging the streets of Toledo.

"Hurry up, young mistress," Sofia urged. "We must still stop off in Butchers' Row. Doña Catarina wants me to buy a slab of mutton and two large hens for your supper on the way home. We should have left Doña Brianda's house earlier."

"And miss having my fortune told? Never!"

"You'll never change, young mistress. You are as full of mischief as when you were a babe." She stopped and adjusted my cloak. "The servants told me that Doña Brianda's slave read your palm. Mara learned her art at her mother's knee on the Dark Continent. What did Mara say?"

"The slave spoke nonsense. She is a foolish girl."

"Don't listen to her then!" She pointed to the left. "Here is Butchers' Row. It won't take long to buy the meat."

The din of the arguing, shouting, bargaining people in Butchers' Row was deafening. I used my right elbow to shove my way through the crowd, and I lifted my skirts with my left hand to keep them out of the sludge on the streets, but it was useless. I gave up and let my skirts drag along the muddy ground while I buried my nose in my sleeve. The smell of blood was heavy in the air. I was overwhelmed by the stink of animal carcasses hanging from hooks in the butchers' stalls and by the stench of unwashed human flesh. My knees buckled and I reached out in front of me to grab Sofia's arm.

"I'm going to be sick!"

She put her arm around my shoulders and helped me over to a stone bench. "Sit here while I conduct my business with Garcia."

I was too busy fighting the gorge rising in my throat to pay attention as she haggled with the young butcher. The argument ended with the transfer of a few coins from Sofia's pocket to the butcher's hand and satisfied smirks on both of their faces.

As the butcher dropped the mutton and hens into Sofia's basket, white and black feathers fluttered up into the air. I tried to catch one, but I wasn't quick enough. The wind blew it away.

With a sigh, Sofia sank to the bench beside me. "How do you feel?"

"A little better."

"Garcia is a thief but no worse than the others," she said. "Your lady mother will be pleased. The meat is very fresh and will make a wonderful stew. Pork would be even better." She scratched her head. "I don't understand why my lady won't let me buy pork. It's less dear and more tender than the old hens and the mutton the butchers peddle."

"Mama says that pork disagrees with her. It gives her pains in her stomach."

"But I could . . ."

Her words were drowned out by the sounding of trumpets. The crowd parted and formed lines on either side of the cobbled street, making way for a procession that had just turned the corner.

"The holy Inquisition!" said a man standing next to me.

His companion crossed herself.

Sofia put down her basket on the ground and both of us stood on the bench to see. In the excitement, I forgot about my queasy stomach. A standard bearer carrying a flag and trumpeting heralds in their crimson and gold were followed by a tall, gaunt man dressed in the white habit and black cloak of a Dominican monk. He was staring straight ahead, holding the green cross of the Inquisition up high.

Sofia bobbed a curtsy as the man passed us.

"Who is he?" I asked. "I've never seen him before."

"Torquemada."

I shuddered. All of Spain knew his name. His holiness, Fray Torquemada, was the Inquisitor General of the holy Inquisition and the confessor of our beloved queen.

Torquemada was followed by four priests clutching crucifixes in their hands and chanting solemnly.

Behind the monks walked a long row of dirty, wretched prisoners. First came a group of women with matted hair and bare feet, dressed in ragged yellow sackcloth tunics – sambenitos. Each sambenito garment had been painted with a crude red cross, front and back.

Next came women in black sambenitos painted

with images of flames pointing downward and grotesque pictures of the devil. They all carried unlit tapered candles in their hands and had tall miters on their heads. Their tall hats should have been comical, but the sight of them made me want to cry.

Behind the female prisoners followed a group of male prisoners, also dressed in yellow and black sambenitos.

A long row of the Inquisition's familiars, its officers, in black clothing trailed the procession.

"Heretics!" cried a woman in front of us. "The pox on you!"

"May your souls rot in hell!" an onlooker taunted the prisoners.

A painfully thin young woman in a black sambenito flinched at his words and pulled the crying baby in her arms closer to her chest. The cheek of the infant rested against the face of the devil on her tunic. The woman's tears intermingled with the tears of her child. I felt my own eyes filling up.

At the front of the group of the male prisoners walked an older man whose dignity shone through his degradation. He held himself straight, as would a soldier leading his men into battle. As he passed us, the butcher Garcia hoisted a bucket of blood and flung it into the man's face. The man wiped his eyes with his sleeve and walked by his tormentor silently, not even glancing at him.

"Heretics!" someone shrieked. "Beg the forgiveness of our Lord and his blessed mother!"

"These poor prisoners," I said to Sofia. "There are so many of them. How can there be so many heretics?"

She looked around carefully. "Hush! You don't want to be overheard asking such questions."

Somebody in the crowd threw a rotten pomegranate at the prisoners. A boy picked up a stone from the ground and pitched it at an old woman in a black sambenito passing by him. Before long, the air was thick with flying stones. The angry barrage did not subside until the procession left Butchers' Row.

Sofia picked up her basket and we set out for home.

"I've seen such a procession once before, when Mama and I went to visit friends. Mama wouldn't answer my questions about the prisoners we saw. She would only say that they were heretics being punished by the Inquisition. She told me to stop asking questions about them, that I was too young to concern myself with such matters. She thinks that I am too young to understand anything!"

Sofia stopped in her tracks, oblivious of the people who bumped into us as they passed, muttering foul curses. "I told you to keep your voice down," she whispered urgently.

"I felt so sorry for the young mother and her babe," I said. "What's going to happen to them?"

"Save your sympathy for those who deserve it."

She spat on the ground, her dark face bristling with hate. It was like looking at a stranger.

"If you must know," she said quietly, "as far as I am concerned, those prisoners, those Marranos, those pigs deserve everything they get! They profane the name of our Lord, Jesus Christ. Those Conversos pretend to worship our Lord but secretly they practice their cursed Jewish customs. They commit heresy against the holy church. The holy Inquisition roots them out and punishes them for their sins. The sambenito, the tunic of shame, is fitting garb for them."

"Why would so many of them profane our Lord? That woman with the baby – she was so young. How could she – "

"No more questions!" Sofia said, hastening her steps so that I had to pick up my skirts and break into a trot to keep up with her.

By the time we arrived at the Bisagra Gate it was late in the afternoon. The gentle breezes felt fresh and cool on my face. Chattering people were waiting their turn to pass through the city gates to leave Toledo for their homes in the countryside. It seemed that every guild was there. A white-haired, wrinkled old woman was harnessed like a donkey to a cart festooned with laces of every kind, selling her wares. A tanner balanced a pole tied with animal skins on his shoulders. A dwarf, dressed in the colorful clothes of a jester, was turning cartwheels in the dust.

Our villa was located not far beyond the gates. Sofia and I didn't speak much as we trudged along the scrubby path to the estate. We saw laborers making their way toward the houses of their masters. Litters on the shoulders of sturdy slaves were transporting fine ladies back to their homes after spending the day visiting friends in Toledo. Cavaliers on horseback kicked up so much dust that it was difficult to breathe. I couldn't get the image of the young mother and her child out of my mind.

Yussuf, the Moorish slave in charge of the other servants in the house, opened the door to us. He bowed deeply.

"Doña Isabel! Welcome home. Your lady mother is asking for you."

"Where is she?"

"Doña Catarina is waiting for you in the rose garden. She asked me to take you to her as soon as you got home."

———

Mama was sitting among the blooms behind the house, her needlework in her lap. Unicorns and courtiers in bright garments were spread over her knees. Her eyes were closed and she was snoring gently.

I kissed her cheek.

She woke with a start. "I must have fallen asleep."

"You did."

"You're home, finally," she said. "I was getting worried. I told Sofia that I wanted you home early. It's unsafe for a maiden to be on the streets of Toledo after dark."

"I know, Mama. We left Brianda's house on time, but we had a long wait at the city gates. There were a lot of people there."

I felt bad about lying, but I had no choice. I didn't want her to be angry with Sofia or with me.

Mama folded her tapestry and stood up.

"I'll go into the house with you," I said. "I want to lie down before supper. I have an aching head."

"An aching head?" She placed her hand over my brow.

"Your forehead is cool. Do you feel any pain? I haven't heard of any new cases of the plague, but we can't be too careful."

"I am fine, Mama. I am just a little tired. What did you want to talk to me about?"

She shaded her eyes with her hand and looked up. The sun had just begun to set, burning up the sky with hidden fire. "It's getting late. We'll talk tomorrow. It's time for your bath."

"I am too tired. I'll bathe tomorrow. I'll be fresher for church on Sunday."

"No! You must bathe tonight before the sun sets."

"Why can't I wait to have my bath until Saturday morning? Why do you always insist that I bathe on Fridays, before sunset? I am old enough to decide what I want to do!"

"So many questions. Just do as you are told."

I could tell by her tone that it was useless to argue with her.

"Your dress is splattered with mud. Please change. You know what your father expects of you." She squinted into the distance as if trying to catch sight of him. "I pray to the good Lord that he'll return safely from his journey, and soon."

Sofia brought two buckets of water up to my room. She warmed up the water in a caldron in the fireplace and then poured it into a metal tub. I lay back in it and closed my eyes, enjoying the warmth.

"Let me help you, young mistress," she said, scrubbing my shoulders with a cloth and easing me forward so she could reach my back. She also washed my hair and helped me dry myself. It took her a few moments to untangle my long, curly, black hair. Twilight was falling by the time we finished. She helped me change into my newest gown. I ran my hands down its skirt. I loved the cool feel of the silky material. Its pink color and gold embroidery warmed my complexion. I knew that I looked my best.

I skipped down the wide staircase that led to the center hall. The large carved wooden table we used for our meals was covered with a velvet cloth and set with metal plates. There were more dishes on the sideboard. There was no sign of Mama. *She probably hasn't finished dressing yet,* I told myself. I decided to go and help her get ready.

The door to Mama's chamber was closed. A muffled sound came from inside. Though I stepped closer, I couldn't hear what she was saying. Every member of our household had strict instructions not to enter my mother's room without knocking first, so I rapped on the door. There was no answer, but the sound ceased. I knocked again, louder.

"It's me, Mama. Let me in!"

"Just a minute."

I heard the key turning in the lock and the door swung open. My mother stood there looking at me. Beside her on a small table I saw two tall tallow candles, their wicks smoky as if they had just been snuffed out.

"Dinner is ready to be served." The smoke made my nose twitch. "Did you just put out those candles? You're always telling me not to use tapers because they cost so much."

"I'll come downstairs in a minute, but first let me arrange your hair." She gathered my curls on top of my head. "You have lovely hair, Isabel, the same curls my mother used to have." She took a white cap out of the armoire and handed it to me. "Put this on."

"You're not answering my question about the candles, Mama," I said while tucking my hair under the cap. "Who were you talking to?"

Sofia appeared in the doorway, breathless. As she curtsied, I saw her looking at the candles with a puzzled expression. "My lady, horsemen are approaching!"

The brush fell out of Mama's hand. She picked up her skirts and hurried past me and out of the room. I followed.

Somebody was banging loudly on the heavy oak door. Yussuf was standing at the door, waiting for instructions. Mama motioned to him to open it. He darted a concerned glance at her before slowly lifting the latches. The door swung open with a creak – and there was Papa! Next to him stood an older cavalier dressed in somber clothes and a boy about my own age. The boy wore gold silk hose, a short blue gown, and a black velvet doublet. A foppish hat covered most of his dark hair. He was a little taller than me and would have been handsome except for the closeness of his dark eyes and the smirk on his lips. He looked at me coldly, as if I were a mare he wanted to buy. Two turbaned Moorish slaves held the horses.

Papa spread his arms wide. I ran into them and he hugged me so hard that all the breath was squeezed out of me. Next it was Mama's turn to be grabbed by the waist and swung around before being carefully set down. Her face was flushed.

"My dear, I am finally home from their majesties' court, and I brought Alfonso de Carrera and his son, Luis, with me. Don Alfonso is their royal highnesses' most trusted advisor. Don Alfonso, Luis, I want you to meet my lady wife Catarina and our daughter, Isabel."

Mama and I both curtsied, and Don Alfonso bowed with a flourish of his hat. Luis nodded frostily.

"Welcome to our home, Don Alfonso, Luis," Mama said. "You must be tired and hungry."

"Rather dirty, too, my lady," Don Alfonso laughed

ruefully, his gaze traveling down his dusty clothes.

Mama nodded to Yussuf. "Show Don Alfonso and his son to the apartment on the third floor. Carry water upstairs and warm it for them to wash. In the meantime," she said, now turning to our guests, "I'll have the servants prepare refreshments for you."

The Moor led Don Alfonso and Luis inside and up the stairs.

Mama ordered Sofia to lay more places at the table. It wasn't long before Mama was plying Don Alfonso and Luis with food. Papa kept refilling their cups with ale. It loosened the cavalier's tongue. At Mama's gentle prodding, he told us about his wife and daughters and described his sprawling estates in the town of Valencia in the Kingdom of Aragon.

"My family is awaiting my return. I'll be honest with you, mistress. I dislike travel, but when I heard your husband's proposition, I told my slaves to saddle our horses and we set out immediately to meet you, Doña Catarina, and your charming daughter," he said with a courtly smile.

Luis remained silent, his expression even more sullen.

"What did Papa suggest to the cavalier?" I whispered to Mama.

She looked daggers at me and I fell silent.

Dinner went on for so long that my eyes kept closing. Mama's elbow in my ribs kept me awake.

When the meal finally ended, Papa ushered Luis and his father to their chambers. I, too, stood up, ready to withdraw to my own bed. Mama motioned for me to remain in my seat.

"Wait for your papa. We have to speak to you."

"What about?"

The solemn expression on her face made my heart beat faster, but she would not explain herself until Papa had returned.

My father clasped my hand when he finally came back downstairs. "I missed you, Isabel," he said. "You have grown into a lovely young woman."

He cleared his throat several times and gave my mother a beseeching look. Finally, she took pity on him.

"What your papa is trying to tell you is that you are a grown woman now, and it is time that you become betrothed," she said. "I was promised to your father when I was your age. Your father and I have chosen Luis to be your future husband."

I stared at them, at a loss for words. I jumped up from my chair. "What do you mean?" I finally croaked. "You promised to wait until I was fifteen! You said that you would pick a boy I liked."

Papa leaned so close that I could smell the ale on his breath. "Sit down, Isabel." His voice was more serious than I had ever heard it before. "I would be remiss in my duties as your father if I did not provide for your safety and comfort in the future."

"But I – "

He held his palm up in the air. "I know what's best for you."

"You promised to – "

"I know what I am doing. Alfonso de Carrera is an Old Christian. His family has followed the Catholic faith for as long as anyone can remember. We live in perilous times. There is no doubt about de Carrera's lineage. Any member of his family is safe from the Inquisition."

"I don't understand you, Papa. Why do we have to fear the Inquisition? They punish heretics, false Christians. We're not like that. We go to church. Nobody is more devout than Mama. I never miss confession with Father Juan."

Papa looked at me intently and opened his mouth as if to speak but then stopped and shook his head.

"Tell her, Enrique! Isabel should know the truth."

"What do you mean?" I asked her.

"Tell her," she repeated.

"What's Mama talking about?"

"Nothing for you to worry about," my father said

impatiently. "I am pleased that you are devout, like Don Alfonso and his family. They would expect Luis's wife to share their faith. Don Alfonso is not only a good Christian. He owns vast, fertile fields and his name is honorable. King Ferdinand consults him regularly on matters of state. However, Don Alfonso's crops have been poor for the past few years and he is having financial problems. I obtained his agreement to a betrothal between you and Luis only after I offered him your very generous dowry. Luis is Don Alfonso's only son. He will inherit his father's estates some day. He will make you an excellent husband. You will be the envy of all who know you."

I grasped his arm. "Let me wait, Papa. You promised that you wouldn't look for a husband for me for another year. That'll give you time to find somebody I'll like more than Luis. I don't want to marry him. He seems arrogant and he has no conversation." My voice rose higher and higher. "I don't like the look of him!"

Papa pried my fingers off his arm, one by one. "You have been indulged, Isabel, and it is my fault. You are my only child and I always gave in to your wishes, but not this time." His voice was stern. "I want what's best for you." He sat down heavily in his chair.

I turned to my mother. "Mama, I beg you, please tell Papa that he is wrong. I don't want to marry Luis. I don't like him!"

"Lower your voice," Mama said. "Your father is not wrong. You can't possibly dislike the boy. You just met him. We know what's best for you. Luis won't be returning with his father to Aragon. He will remain in Toledo so that the two of you can get to know each other. He will make you a good husband. You must do your duty."

"But Mama – "

She cut off my words with a wave of her hand. "The marriage ceremony will not take place until you turn fifteen. You will be used to the idea of marrying him by then."

I fell to my knees, my hands clasped in front of me. "Please, Papa! Please, Mama! I beseech you. Don't do this to me!"

My mother turned her head. My father twirled his cup around in his hands, over and over again, but would not meet my eyes.

"The betrothal ceremony will be one week hence," he said.

CHAPTER 2

MONDAY, NOVEMBER 14, 1491 –
SUNDAY, NOVEMBER 20, 1491

No matter how hard I tried, I could not change my parents' minds, so I decided to follow Mama's advice. I told myself that Luis was actually quite handsome, except for the meanness of his eyes. Perhaps if I gave him a chance and got to know him, I might grow to like him.

The rose garden was a riot of color. Red, yellow, and white roses lined our path. Wild, rambling roses climbed up the stone walls that enclosed the garden, their sweet scent overwhelming.

"My mama spends much of her time with the flowers," I told Luis as we wandered down one of the paths leading to an arboretum in the center of the garden. Sofia was chaperoning us, following behind, out of earshot. "Does your mother have a garden, too?"

Luis snickered. "Indeed, she does. Like all women, my mother devotes too much of her time to frivolous pursuits. I will make sure that any wife of mine will not waste her time in such a manner. There are more important things a wife should do – such as supervising the lazy servants for her husband's comfort and providing heirs to her lord's property."

"But the flowers are so beautiful – "

His cold look silenced me.

We walked beside each other without speaking until a small salamander ran across the path. It must have been a baby for it was very small. It stopped on the path directly in front of us.

I picked up my skirts, ready to step over it, when Luis stomped on the poor creature with the heel of his boot. The little animal writhed in pain. Luis kept stomping and stomping on its body until it stopped quivering. He finally kicked it off the walk, into the bushes.

I began to tremble. "Why did you kill it? It did you no harm!"

"I hate those slimy creatures," he said in a self-satisfied voice.

I no longer could bear to spend more time in his company. I shaded my eyes with my hand and looked at the sky. "It's getting late. I must bid you good-bye. My parents are awaiting me."

He shrugged his shoulders. I could see that he didn't care that I wanted to leave. "As you wish."

Before I could move, he turned on his heels and knocked against me. Suddenly I felt his cruel fingers pinching my breast.

"Ouch! How dare you."

Sofia ran toward us. I did not wait for her. I slapped his grinning face with all my might.

He stepped closer and grabbed my wrist. His fingers were like a vice, but I stood my ground. "You will soon find out how much I dare!" he snarled. "You will pay dearly for your behavior, my lady."

He made a deep, exaggerated bow and strode off toward the house. I hurried, almost running, down the path in the opposite direction to meet Sofia.

Once we were safely through the garden gate, we leaned against it to talk about what had just happened. Sofia handed me a handkerchief and I wiped away my tears.

"He is no good," she said, gesturing in Luis's direction with her head. "He whips his slaves. You better tell your papa what he is like."

Papa would not listen to me. I begged, I cajoled, I raged – but to no avail. My father was deaf to my pleas.

"You are innocent of the ways of the world. Luis is no different from other men. I know what's best for you," he said. "The betrothal must take place."

Mama took Papa's side. She repeated constantly: "You must do your duty. The boy will make you a good husband. You will get used to his ways."

I knew *that* would never happen, but she would not listen when I told her that Luis had an unkind heart. "He kills living things for no reason, Mama. You are the one who taught me never to hurt defenseless creatures."

She would not relent.

I was so embarrassed that I could not bring myself to tell her about his lack of respect toward me. Instead, I tried to explain that the perfumes he used to cover the odor of his unwashed body sickened me. No matter what I said, she ignored my words.

I soon realized that there was nothing I could do to change my parents' minds. I became determined to stay as far away from Luis as possible.

Finally, the day I had dreaded arrived – the day of my betrothal. The golden warmth of the sun woke me up. I lay in my bed, still drowsy, until I remembered what day it was. I rang for Sofia. She wept with me as she got me ready. Both of us knew that I had no choice, that there was no escape. I had to obey my parents.

She bathed me and helped me into a chemise and kirtle. Above it I wore a blue gown embroidered in the colors of the rainbow. The flowing, long skirt made me feel grown-up. The blue color emphasized my purity, and the richness of the embroidery my position in society. She coiled my hair at the nape of my neck and covered it with a snood embroidered with gold thread. Finally, she rubbed a salve made of berries and spices over my cheeks to give them a rosy glow. She painted my lips with the same potion.

Mama entered my room, most handsome in green silk.

"You look beautiful," she said.

"So do you."

She pulled me close to her, as if to kiss me. Before I realized what she was doing, she plucked several hairs from my hairline.

I jumped back. "What are you doing? Why are you hurting me?"

She laughed. "Now you have a noble brow, like our queen, for whom you are named." She took my hand and twirled me around. "Perfect! Luis will be mad with passion for you."

I sank to my knees. "Please stop this charade, Mama. I beg you. I don't want to become Luis's bride."

"That's for your father and me to decide," she said in a stern voice I rarely heard from her. She sat down on a stool, careful to spread her skirts around her. "By marrying Luis, you will strengthen your position at the royal court, and – most importantly – you will be safe from the Inquisition."

"Why do I have to strengthen my position at court? Papa is their majesties' favorite physician. He can do no wrong in their eyes. We have no reason to fear the Inquisition. We are good Catholics."

Mama rose from her seat with a whisper of her skirts. "Again, too many questions, my girl. I must go to the kitchen to check on preparations for the food. The guests will expect a feast after the betrothal ceremony." She patted my hand. "Go for a walk. It will calm your nerves."

I found myself by the orange tree that grew beside the house. From where I sat I could see anyone coming, and the leaves hid me from prying eyes. I stretched my arms and legs wide and leaned against the trunk of the tree. I closed my eyes to try to take in the smells and sounds of this garden, my childhood playground.

I must have dozed off, because before I knew it, the clopping of hooves startled me awake. A boy, riding a mule, was arriving at our front door. A large package wrapped in rags was slung over the mule, in front of his saddle. Quickly, I got to my feet and went to meet him.

He was a tall boy, a little older than me, with swarthy skin and wild, black curls partially covered by the pointed hood of his long cloak. The badge Jews had to wear, a white circle with a smaller red circle inside it, was sewn onto the left shoulder of his garment.

"Whoa! Where did you come from?" he asked.

I didn't answer.

He pointed to the orange tree. "Were you hiding behind that tree?"

"Who are you? What do you want?"

"I am Yonah, the son of Natan Abenatar, the master silversmith," he said proudly. "I am delivering a centerpiece for a table." He nodded at the package in front of him. "I was told that it was needed for the betrothal meal in honor of the daughter of the house. Where should I take it?" He climbed off his mule with easy grace.

"Come with me." I made my voice as haughty as I could.

The slight smile on his lips made me wonder if he was laughing at me. I looked around. There was no sign of Yussuf. He was most likely in the kitchen, driving the servants wild with his demands.

"Yes, my lady." The slight tremor in his voice made me look at him more closely. I still couldn't decide if he was making fun of me.

I led him through the house into the grand hall. There were flowers everywhere in large pottery vases. The table in the center of the room was set with silver dishes.

"This is a beautiful room," he said, his eyes roaming over the rich carpets and wall hangings depicting knights rescuing damsels in distress. "Where would you like me to put the centerpiece?"

He undid the rags to reveal a golden skylark in a silver cage. The bird's feathers were ruffled and he seemed poised for flight. His gold eyes seemed to sparkle, as if in the ecstasy of his song. I could actually hear his trilling notes in my imagination. Somehow, the bird also seemed frightened and sad. His silver cage was intricately carved with different kinds of silver fruits hanging over the bars – oranges, grapes, and pomegranates.

I stuck my fingers through the cage and touched the bird's golden feathers. "This bird is beautiful. A masterpiece! He looks alive. I can almost hear his song. He wants to fly away. He wants to be free."

The boy smiled at me. I smiled back.

"Thank you," he said. "My father and I spent many happy hours with this little creature." He patted the bird's head with calloused fingers. "I am happy that he will belong to somebody who'll appreciate his grace and spirit."

He turned toward the door. There was something so honest and so compelling about him.

I didn't want him to leave. "What did you say your name was?"

"Yonah. What do they call you?"

I didn't know how to reply. Should I berate him for his boldness? After all, I was Isabel, daughter of Enrique de Cardosa, the queen's physician. Who was he but a simple silversmith and a despised Jew? How dare he speak to me as an equal? Despite this, my mouth seemed to have a will of its own.

"I am Isabel. The bird you made is for the table at the banquet in honor of my betrothal."

An expression I could not fathom flittered over his face. "I wish you much happiness, Isabel," he said.

Tears welled up in my eyes. "Happiness is not my fate. My parents are forcing me to marry a boy I detest. He is unkind, with a heart of ice."

"Do your parents know how you feel?"

I brushed away my tears angrily. "They won't listen to me. I don't understand why."

There was a loud noise outside. He put a finger to his lips. Several servants carrying crockery in their arms charged into the hall. He bowed and walked out of the room.

The sun was still hot despite the lateness of the day as Luis and I stood in front of the chapel door. My parents were on my right. Luis's father stood on his left. The rolled-up betrothal contract, describing my dowry in detail, was clutched in Don Alfonso's hand. Friends and relatives crowded around us. Brianda was standing with her parents at the back; she gave me a loving smile. Father Juan, who had officiated at my christening, joined Luis's hand and mine.

"Do you, Luis de Carrera, swear a solemn oath that you wish to be betrothed to Isabel, the daughter of Enrique de Cardosa?"

"I do," Luis said.

"Do you, Isabel de Cardosa, wish to be betrothed to Luis, the son of Alfonso de Carrera?"

I looked at Papa. His features were set in stone. Mama nodded her head when my eyes turned toward her. I could hear whispers all around me.

"Do you, Isabel de Cardosa, wish to be betrothed to Luis, the son of Alfonso de Carrera?" Father Juan repeated in a louder voice.

I lowered my head. "I do."

"The marriage between Luis de Carrera and Isabel de Cardosa will take place a year from this day unless both parties agree to the dissolution of this betrothal contract for a just cause prior to that date," announced Father Juan. He turned to Luis. "You and your lady are now betrothed. You may kiss her."

Luis lowered his head, his eyes gleaming darkly. His lips were cold and wet against my cheek. "You will learn who your master is very soon," he whispered.

I looked away to escape his gloating eyes.

The guests were greeting one another and laughing heartily. I blinked away the tears in my eyes. Several ladies embraced me. Brianda took my arm while my other friends danced around me as we made our way toward the house. The young cavaliers congratulated Luis with claps on his back and winks at me. Musicians in colorful garb plucked lutes and shook jingling tambourines as we walked. The high-pitched sound of a lonely flute pierced the clear sky. A young woman sang sweetly.

> In love, my mother,
> In love I fell asleep.
> Thus asleep I dreamt
> Of what keeps my heart awake.
> That love comforts me
> With a goodness I do not deserve.

Gradually, the other revelers joined in the song. As I led this happy procession, I felt numb, as if I was looking at the events around me from a place far, far away.

Mama hugged me. "We're doing this for your own good, for your safety," she said quietly. "You will thank us."

I did not answer her.

At the house, the boisterous guests claimed their seats at the banquet table laden with all kinds of delicacies. They ate quail, goose, and oysters steamed in almond sauce. They tore at roasted peacock, mutton, and boar. They clinked their cups filled with ale or spicy mulled wine and washed away its taste with the sweetness of wild pears. I forced myself to take a little fruit. Each mouthful choked me.

The musicians played their songs, but the guests didn't pay them much attention while they ate. By the end of the meal, though, the young men and women formed a circle and began to turn and dip to the musicians' plaintive tune.

Let us eat and drink today,
And sing and rejoice.
Since tomorrow we will have to fast,
Let's please ourselves today.

Suddenly, I couldn't bear the gaiety any longer. I whispered to Mama that I had to use my chamber pot and rushed out of the hall. I made my way toward the staircase, quiet as a ghost, my silk slippers whispering against the tiled floor. I had to pass a room the servants usually used. Its door was open a crack and I heard two people talking. I recognized Sofia's voice. I heard my name spoken, and I stopped.

"Isabel is far too gentle and kind for your young master," Sofia said. "Luis is cruel and has roving hands."

"At least he is of pure blood, unlike the Converso mongrel you serve every day," replied a gruff male voice I did not know.

"How dare you speak with such a lack of respect for my young mistress!" Sofia spat back. "Isabel is a fine lady, as is her mother, Doña Catarina. That's more than I can say of your master with his crude ways."

The man laughed. "At least Luis is an Old Christian and not the whelp of cursed Marranos. Doña Catarina and Don Enrique, they probably still worship in their Jew religion secretly."

"You lie!" Sofia shrieked.

"Mark my words," the man said, "the Inquisition will come for your fine mistress one day. She is lucky that Luis is willing to marry her – he was lured in by her large dowry."

"That's not true! My lady goes to church – "

I heard footsteps approaching the door, so I picked up my skirts and ran up the stairs as fast as I could.

I sat down on the edge of my bed, repeating to myself what I had just learned. Why did the man call us Marranos? A marrano was a pig. Why did he say that we were Conversos, New Christians? Our family has served the mother church forever. He accused us of practicing Jewish customs. I didn't even know any Jews – except Yonah. And I had just met him.

Mama knocked softly and came into my chamber.

"Come down to the banquet immediately. It is a great insult to Luis and his father if their future wife and new daughter disappears."

"I have to ask you a question first."

"Later! Everybody awaits you downstairs."

One look at her determined face convinced me to wait.

CHAPTER 3

SUNDAY, NOVEMBER 20, 1491

The betrothal feast was finally over.

"I have to talk to you. And to Papa, too," I whispered in Mama's ear.

She glanced at me before turning back to the guests bidding her good-bye. After a few minutes, only Luis and his father were left behind. Alfonso de Carrera was in conversation with my father at the table again, and Luis was slumped over the table, deep in his cups.

"It's time for us to return to our chambers," Don Alfonso finally said, pushing himself up from the table. "Come, son. We have to go to bed."

He slapped Luis on the back. Luis groaned but didn't stir. Don Alfonso grabbed a fistful of Luis's hair and lifted his head off the table. "We have to go!" he yelled into Luis's face.

Luis's head dropped back to the table with a bang when his father let go.

"The boy celebrated his betrothal too vigorously," Don Alfonso said with a lascivious smile. He slapped his thigh in merriment. "Wait until he celebrates his wedding night!"

I swallowed hard. Sofia had told me of the things that newlyweds did on that night, after Mama had refused to answer my questions.

Don Alfonso beckoned to two of the Moorish slaves standing against the wall. "Take the boy," he ordered.

Each slave put one of Luis's arms around his neck and dragged my betrothed out of the room, leaving behind a trail of drool.

After much bowing and protestations of kinship, Don Alfonso followed them.

Mama leaned against the table. "Finally! I didn't think that they'd ever leave. I am so weary. I must go to my bed before I fall asleep on my feet."

I tugged at her sleeve. "I told you that I have to talk to you and to Papa . . . without strange ears near us." I nodded toward the servants, who had begun to clear the table.

"Can it wait until tomorrow? I am tired."

"No, Mama. It can't. I must speak to you. Now."

She sighed and dismissed the slaves with a wave of

her hand. "What's the matter, Isabel? What's so important?"

"I have heard something that frightened me. Sofia was arguing with one of Luis's servants."

"So?"

"Wait, Mama. I am coming to it. The man she was talking to said that I was fortunate that Luis was willing to marry me, even with my large dowry, because we are Marranos. A marrano is a swine. He said that we were pigs, Mama! Why would he call us such an awful name? He also said that we were Conversos, New Christians."

"Hush!" Mama cried. She ran to the door and slammed it shut. "Keep your voice down. The servants might hear you." She put her hands on her hips and berated Papa. "I hope that you are pleased with yourself, Enrique. You wouldn't listen to me when I told you that Isabel should know the truth."

"I thought that it was safer for her not to know, but if the servants are gossiping, we don't have a choice. Everybody must know." Papa turned to me. "We have to explain our situation to you."

Mama sat down at the table with Papa and me. Both of them stared at me intently for a long moment. Mama clasped my hand and she rested her head on my shoulder. My heart began to race.

"My daughter, my only child, you are more precious to me and to your lady mother than all the untold riches that are hidden in the Indies far, far, away. It pains me that I must have this conversation with you – "

"Papa – "

He held up his hand. "Be patient, my daughter, and listen carefully." He cleared his throat. "I don't even know where to begin."

"Start at the beginning," Mama said tartly. "Just tell her."

"The beginning . . . as good a place as any. I am sorry to tell you that we are not who you thought we were. Both your mother's grandparents and my grandparents were Jewish. I wish that you could have met them. They were wonderful people."

All the breath squeezed out of me. Our family Jewish! How could that be? I knew very little about Jews. They were an accursed, greedy race forced to wear a round red and white badge that exposed them to the world's contempt. All who knew them despised them.

"This can't be true! Being a good Catholic means that we'll go to heaven. We never miss church on Sunday. You've always said how important it is to pay close attention to Father Juan during my catechism lessons. I've never even met any Jewish people – except the silversmith's son, who delivered this beautiful bird." I gestured at the golden skylark warbling his unheard song.

Mama leaned closer. "We are descended from the ten lost tribes of Israel," she said. "Our grandparents were forcibly converted to Christianity at the point of a sword. It was either death or the acceptance of Jesus Christ. They chose life."

"Forgive us for not telling you, but try to understand," Papa said. "I felt that the less you knew, the safer it was for you. We live in perilous times. The Inquisition is ready to accuse New Christians, like us, of heresy in order to gain control of our property. They hate us. As you heard, they call us Marranos, swine. The Inquisition's familiars are everywhere, ready to lay false charges against us. We must be careful. We can't trust anyone."

"We've never forgotten the old ways of the God of Abraham and of Moses," Mama said. "We still worship the one and only God, the God of our forefathers, blessed be his name," she added, her voice trembling. "In our hearts, we are still Jewish!"

"How *can* you be? Everybody knows that Jews are loathsome, evil creatures."

As soon as the words slipped out of my mouth, I thought of Yonah. He seemed so honest and so kind. He tried to help me during my moment of despair.

Would an evil person do that? Why was he so different from the rest of his people?

Mama began to cry. "What have we done? What have we done?" She hid her face in her hands, frightening me even more. "Our daughter detests her own kind!"

Papa patted her knee before resting his arm around my shoulders. "Don't believe the lies you hear, Isabel," he said somberly. "Our people are no better and no worse than anybody else. Our only crime is that we are still waiting for the Messiah."

"Do Luis and his father know that we are New Christians?"

Papa shrugged his shoulders. "I never told them, but if the servants are gossiping about it, they must."

"There are many Conversos in our beloved kingdom, which our people call Sefarad," Mama said. "Some Conversos are devout Christians. But others, like us, follow the old ways secretly, away from the prying eyes of the Inquisition. Luis and his father certainly don't know that." Her face softened. "It would give me the greatest pleasure to teach you about the religion of the Jewish people, as my mother taught me."

"But, Mama, I – "

"No more questions," Papa interrupted. "We've told you enough for now. I can't bear another second of this." He ran his fingers through his hair. "We'll talk more tomorrow. I don't have to tell you that no mention of our secret should ever pass your lips. Only a handful of trusted friends know of our Jewish background. Our lives may depend upon your silence."

Chapter 4

Monday, November 21, 1491 –
Friday, November 25, 1491

The tall trees obscured the sun. The howling of wild beasts made the hair on the back of my neck stand up. Suddenly, the trees around me burst into flame. The fire encircled me. There was no escape. I cried for help. Suddenly – hoofbeats. Luis appeared astride a black steed. He galloped through the fire and drew in his reins. His horse reared on its hind legs. I held out my arms toward Luis. He laughed, whipped his animal, and then he was gone. The flames were coming closer and closer . . . I awoke covered in sweat.

I felt so weighed down by the events of the previous day that I couldn't move. I was betrothed. Betrothed to a boy I detested. And I belonged to a people doomed to burn in hell for eternity because they didn't believe in Jesus. Would I still go to heaven or would I have to share their fate? I believed in the Lord Jesus with my whole being, and I attended mass regularly. Surely our Lord's beloved mother would protect me and keep me safe.

With a heavy heart I climbed out of bed, walked to the corner of my room, and fell to my knees in front of a statue of the Virgin Mary. The blessed mother's alabaster eyes looked on me with compassion. I prayed to the Virgin to help me, and to help Mama and Papa, too. I asked her to give us health and happiness. I prayed for eternal salvation.

Sofia came into the room. Her rough fingers began to smooth down my hair.

"Young mistress, why didn't you ring for me?"

"I am praying to the Virgin."

"It's time to get dressed." She helped me up from the floor. "I'll get your clothes for you." She began to pull garments out of the armoire. "I would have come up to your room sooner, but my lady wanted me to stay with the silversmith's son while he was repairing her broken jewelry in the kitchen. Yussuf was busy with other tasks."

"Repairing Mama's jewelry?"

"Her ladyship says that the Jew is skillful. He proved it with the golden bird he made for your betrothal. He is still in the kitchen – working on a bracelet for your lady mother."

Yonah, in my house. How I wanted to see him!

Sofia helped me put on a chemise and kirtle, and she slipped a gown over my head. Grumbling, she did up the hooks at the back. Next, she coiled my hair and pulled a coif over it. When she finally finished, she stepped back.

"There! You look lovely, young mistress," she said. "I'll tidy up while you pick the jewelry you want to wear today."

She turned her back to me and bent over my bed to straighten the linens. I took my wooden jewelry chest out of the armoire. I always kept the box locked. I made sure that Sofia was still turned away before I stood on my tiptoes and reached into a vase that stood on top of the armoire. I found the key inside.

I unlocked the chest, took out the heavy gold chain my parents had given me for my confirmation, locked the chest, and put the key back in its hiding place. Sofia was still busy. I tugged the chain with all my might. It took several tries, but the clasp finally gave way.

"Oh no! Look what happened when I tried to close the clasp of this necklace. It broke."

"What a pity. It's such a beautiful chain. Give it to me." She took it out of my hand. "The silversmith's son is still downstairs. I'll take it to him. He'll repair it."

"No! Bring the boy to me. This chain is one of my favorites. I want to ask him how he plans to fix it."

She returned the gold chain to me and went to fetch Yonah. I pinched my cheeks and bit my lips to make them rosier. I sat down on a stool facing the door, careful to spread out my skirts.

Yonah bowed deeply. "My lady, your servant tells me that you have a broken necklace."

Not with a blink did he let on that we knew each other.

"Yes, I do." I kept my voice haughty. I turned to Sofia. "I just remembered . . . I forgot my fan on a bench in the rose garden. Fetch it for me."

Sofia's eyes darted to Yonah. I could see that she was reluctant to leave me alone with a young man.

"I'll ask one of the kitchen maids," she said. "I'll be back in a moment."

Yonah stepped closer. "How are you?"

"Better. I wanted to thank you for listening to me the other day." I lowered my voice. "We must speak quickly. I broke the clasp on the necklace on purpose. I want to talk to you. Meet me by the orange tree tomorrow night, after sunset."

I could feel the heat rising in my cheeks and couldn't meet his eyes. I hoped that he didn't think that I was too forward.

"I'll be there!" he whispered.

There were footsteps outside my door.

"It won't be difficult to repair the gold chain, my lady," he said as Sofia returned.

I threw a dark cloak over my nightdress and tiptoed down the corridor. The house was so quiet that I could hear my own breathing. My feet were bare – I didn't want to make any sound. As I passed the open door of the kitchen, I could see Sofia's sleeping form in front of the fireplace. She turned restlessly on the pallet she used as her bed. I held my breath as her snores rose to a deafening crescendo, but she didn't open her eyes.

The latches that secured the door rattled as loudly as cannons when I undid them with trembling fingers.

I slipped into the garden. The clouds had hidden the moon, and I had to run my fingers along the wall of the house to guide me as I made my way around it. Though I had walked it countless times, in the dark it seemed strange and new.

The fragrance of the oranges hanging from the boughs sweetened the air. A figure clad in dark clothing stepped out from behind the trunk of the tree, making me jump. A cloud danced away from the moon, reveal-ing Yonah's face.

"I was afraid that you wouldn't come," he whispered.

"I had to wait until everybody was asleep."

He was standing so close that I could feel his breath on my face.

"Tell me about your betrothal," he said.

We sat down on the ground under the heavy boughs and I recounted the events of the last few days. I even told him how the memory of Luis's lips on my cheek sent a chill down my spine. The words tumbled out of my mouth. I could not stop them any more than I could have stopped the flow of a river. Then, I found myself repeating what Mama and Papa had told me. The minute the words escaped my lips I wished that I could take them back. My parents had made it very clear that their secret was not mine to share.

It was as if Yonah could read my mind. "Your secret is safe with me. I understand now why I felt as if I had always known you the minute my eyes fell upon your face. You are one of us."

I swept away a tear. I was happy that the darkness covered my distress.

"I don't know where I belong," I said. "I have always believed in the Lord Jesus. Now . . . I don't know what I am supposed to believe."

"You belong to God's chosen people. You are one

of us," he repeated. "It is your duty to discover this. I will help you do it."

I looked into his eyes. "How?"

"Do you know anything about being Jewish?"

I shook my head. "Nothing. You are the first person of the Jewish faith I have ever met. Your people keep apart."

"We have no choice. But it wasn't always so. My father told me that Jews, Christians, and Muslims lived peacefully side by side for centuries in our kingdom. We were good neighbors and all the children played together. We respected each other's beliefs and traditions. All that has been wiped away during the last hundred years. The Christians became our masters. They made slaves of the Muslims. They converted some Jews to Christianity by the sword. The rest of us were forced into ghettos, called *Juderias*. We had no choice. We still don't. We must still live in them."

"I've seen Jews with red and white badges on the streets, but I have never spoken to one of your race."

"*Our* race?"

I didn't know how to reply. Was I really one of those Jews . . . reviled and hated by all and doomed to go to hell? How could that be? After all, I was Doña Isabel, the daughter of the queen's favorite physician, respected and admired by everyone. "You are mistaken, Yonah. I have nothing in common with your people!" I stood up and dusted off my skirts. "I must go."

"Think about what I've told you," he called after me. "I can help you to become one of us."

I clamped my hands over my ears to shut out his voice, but I couldn't shut out the thoughts crowding my head as I fumbled my way back to my chamber. I did want to learn about my family's old religion, but if I did, would I be punished with eternal damnation for my curiosity? I couldn't forget about the young woman and her baby marching to their deaths in the dreadful procession I'd witnessed. If the Inquisitors discovered my interest in the old ways, would I share the girl's fate – or even worse?

Safe in my room, I dropped to my knees, as I always did when anything disturbed me. I prayed to the Virgin for guidance. I prayed for her to help me make the right decision.

The choice was taken out of my hands. Mama and Papa began to talk about the old religion, and they would not stop. It was as if the dam that had held water back finally broke, allowing it to gush out unchecked. My mother's eyes were filled with joy and my father's with pride when they spoke of their heritage. Their words made their way into my heart. Whenever the panic and fear rose in me, I forced myself not to think about what could happen to us. I didn't reveal my friendship with Yonah and how he, too, wanted to teach me the old ways. I wanted to tell them about him, but I was frightened that they would forbid me to see him. Not only was he a Jew, but he was also just a silversmith's son. They would say that he was inferior to me in every way. I told myself that I didn't care.

I was up late every night, my mind teeming with questions I couldn't answer. Who was I? What did I believe? When exhaustion finally drove me to fitful sleep, I dreamed of church, of the familiar smell of incense that made me feel at home, of the dry taste of the host in my mouth when I took communion, and of the sharpness of the wine when I drank our savior's blood. I imagined singing the hymns that made my heart soar during mass.

Five long days and nights passed before I came to a decision. I summoned Sofia to my room and ordered her to go to the Juderia. Her eyebrows rose, but she remained silent.

"I want you to find me Yonah, son of Natan Abenatar, the master silversmith, and tell him that I will meet him tonight in the same place where we met before."

Her mouth fell open. "Young mistress, what are you saying? Surely you did not meet a young man – and, to make it worse, one of that cursed Jewish race – without taking me along with you? Your lady mother will have me flogged when she finds out what you have done!"

"She will never find out if neither you nor I tell her."

Sofia walked to the door, dragging her feet.

"But, my lady, I've never been to the Juderia. What if the Jews kill me and use my blood to make their Easter bread?" She spat on the floor. "A pox on them!"

I threw my shoe at her. "Don't talk like that! Be gone with you and do as you are told."

From that day onward, Yonah and I met under the branches of the orange tree several times every week. On the days that we arranged to see each other, I waited and waited impatiently for night to fall. It wasn't long before I couldn't imagine life without him. How wrong I had been to believe that he was a simple servant. I discovered that not only was he a skilled craftsman who learned how to transform gold and silver into beautiful objects at his father's knee, but that he was also a scholar. Every evening, he and his father studied the Torah, the Five Books of Moses in the Hebrew Bible. He told me of our ancestors. He spoke of Abraham, who was ready to sacrifice his son for the glory of God;

of Esther, who saved her people by marrying a king; and of Yonah, who was swallowed by a whale.

I asked him about his family.

"I have the best father in the world. He is patient and kind with never a harsh word for me. He is always ready to listen to my problems."

His face was full of sadness.

"What's the matter?"

He sighed. "The Lord took away my mama in childbirth five years ago, when I was eleven years old. Nor was my baby brother long for this world. I miss them so much. It's only my papa and me now."

My heart was so filled with pity that I did the unthinkable. I reached over and clasped his hands in mine.

"Isabel!"

He was as shocked as I was.

My fingers tightened. As I felt the warmth of his hand, the coursing of his blood, I began to feel a kinship that I had never felt before. We sat silently listening to the sounds of the night. A toad croaked. The grass rustled as a mouse scurried among the blades.

Sofia came for me while I was searching for the gold ribbon that Papa had given me. Mama had ordered me to wear it in my hair. Luis was coming for dinner.

"I want him to see how pretty you are," she said.

I didn't bother answering her.

The ribbon wasn't in the armoire or in the wooden chest at the foot of my bed.

"Young mistress, Doña Catarina is getting impatient," Sofia said. "She asked me to tell you to come downstairs immediately. She is waiting for you in the dining hall, as is Don Enrique. Don Luis will be arriving very soon."

"Tell my mother that I'll be there in a minute."

My maid left. I looked in my workbox, but the ribbon wasn't there either, so I gave up. My parents did not like to be kept waiting. Nor did I want to make them angry.

I skipped down the staircase, two steps at a time, and ran straight into Luis.

"Whoa, my lady!" he said, grabbing me by the waist. His fingers lingered too long. "What's your hurry?"

"My parents are waiting for me, my lord. And for you, too."

I tried to pull away, but he wouldn't let go.

"Where have you been, my pretty? I haven't seen you for days."

"I've been busy, my lord."

"Then make yourself less busy. You must learn how to treat your master."

He finally released me. How I wished that I could swipe the smirk off his lips. I curtsied and hurried away. I heard him chuckling as he followed me. I felt unclean.

CHAPTER 5

THURSDAY, DECEMBER 1, 1491

Tia Juana's house stood inside the stone walls of Toledo. Although she wasn't my aunt by blood, I called Doña Juana *tia* because I had known and loved her all my life. She was my godmother and Mama's oldest friend, just as her daughter Brianda was now my oldest friend.

Mama and I sat in the litter, with Papa between us. Yussuf followed the litter, jostling his way through the crowded street.

At Tia Juana's house, the bearers lowered the litter to the ground. We got out just as a trumpet fanfare sounded sharp and clear. The crowd parted to make way for a horseman clad in the white vestments and black cloak of a Dominican monk. I recognized him immediately. It was Fray Torquemada, the Inquisitor General, surrounded by his familiars. The Inquisition's men wore black with the white cross of Saint Dominic stitched on their cloaks, their swords dangling at the sides of their black horses. As the Grand Inquisitor passed through the crowd, onlookers doffed their caps. The men bowed and the women curtsied as if to a king. Several people even crossed themselves.

As Torquemada approached our little party, an urchin darted out of the crowd and startled his horse. The Grand Inquisitor's great steed reared and pawed the air, but Torquemada held on. I jumped backward. He calmed the horse easily, and one of the familiars grabbed the bridle. Another of Torquemada's men picked up the unfortunate boy by the scruff of his neck and dragged him away kicking and screaming. The child could not have been more than eight years of age. Not a sound of protest came from the crowd.

Torquemada noticed us. "Don Enrique, I didn't know that you were back in Toledo, that you had left the royal court." His voice was thin and raspy.

Papa swept off his hat, bowing with a flourish. "Greetings, your excellency! Their majesties were in great spirits and even better health, so I was able to come home to see my wife and daughter."

"This is your wife and daughter?" His voice was cold.

Mama and I curtsied, but he didn't address us. A shiver ran down my spine as his eyes swept over me.

"I hope that your excellency is well," Papa said.

"Except for dropsy," Torquemada replied in a petulant tone. "I suffer from it mightily." He pulled in his reins. "I must bid you good-bye now, Don Enrique. The holy Inquisition needs my humble efforts."

Papa bowed again as Torquemada spurred his horse. The crowd buzzed with excitement.

Mama clutched Papa's arm. "He must know," she said, "or he wouldn't have singled you out. He isn't famous for his social graces."

"Silence, Catarina!" Papa hissed.

"Know what? What must Fray Torquemada know?" Mama hushed me.

"Let's go inside," Papa said, pulling the iron bell at the door of Tia Juana's house.

Papa left for the tavern to attend a cockfight, but he had promised to return for us in an hour. Yussuf was in the kitchen with the servants. Mama and I were chatting with Doña Juana and Brianda as we rested on the embroidered pillows strewn over the fine carpet. I felt drowsy and content, and thoughts of Yonah's dark eyes filled my head. I was planning to meet him under our tree after the sun had set.

"What is troubling you, Catarina?" Doña Juana looked at Mama with her kind eyes.

"It was awful. We saw Torquemada outside your door. A boy darted out and startled his horse. His familiars dragged the boy away. I don't know what will become of him, but one thing is certain. That poor child won't be heard of again." She fanned herself.

"But the boy deserved to be punished," Tia Juana retorted. "He might have injured his holiness!"

"Holiness?" Mama asked, incredulous.

"Yes, holiness," Tia Juana said brusquely. "That man is a saint. Did you know that he wears a hair shirt under his vestments? That he won't eat any but the simplest of foods? He works so hard! If misfortune befell him, what would happen to the holy Inquisition? But I guess that with your background, neither you nor Enrique care."

Mama closed her fan with a snap. She tapped it against her chin. "What exactly do you mean, Juana?" she finally asked.

Tia Juana shrugged her shoulders. "Never mind. I know that – "

The drapes over the doorway parted and Mara glided into the room, which silenced Tia Juana. I hadn't seen Brianda's slave since the day she told me my fortune. Her hair was covered by an embroidered scarf and her eyes were modestly lowered. She was carrying a large silver tray laden with almond cakes. She passed them around the room. I took two cakes. They were so sweet. I sighed contentedly as I washed them down with the juice of freshly squeezed oranges from Tia Juana's orchards.

"I must get the recipe for this cake from your cook, Juana," Mama said. "It's absolutely delicious. Much better than the ones my servants bake."

"That's because you are too lax with them, Catarina," Tia Juana said. "Be firm with them. Let them know that you won't accept anything but the best from them." She softened her words with a smile. "I am glad that you like the cakes. I'll get the recipe for you before you leave." She motioned to the slave girl hovering by the wall. "Mara, more cake for Doña Catarina."

The girl approached Mama with downcast eyes and offered the tray for her inspection. Mama took a second cake. I took my third. Brianda reached for a cake, too, but Tia Juana tapped her hand with her fan.

"Put it down! You are too plump. Your father will never find you a husband."

Brianda's face turned crimson. She glared at Tia

Juana sulkily and threw the cake back at the tray. The cake missed its mark and fell to the carpet, where it crumbled into several pieces.

"Look what you've done, Mara. You're so clumsy!" she screamed.

Mara cowered. Brianda leaned forward and pinched the slave's arm. The girl's eyes glistened with tears, but she remained silent. She crouched down to pick up the pieces from the carpet. Before she could finish, Brianda jumped up, trampling the crumbs under her velvet slippers.

Tia Juana did not utter a single word. Mama's lips were pressed together tightly. I knew that she would have plenty to say if I ever spoke to Sofia the way Brianda treated her slave.

"Let's go to my chamber," Brianda suggested, pulling me up from the floor. "I want to show you the necklace Father gave me."

I picked up the necklace from the table and walked over to the window to dangle it from my fingers in the sunlight streaming into the room. I had never seen anything like it. It was made of gold so fine that it seemed to have been spun from a glittering cobweb.

"Try it on," Brianda said. She took it out of my hand

and draped it around my neck, fastening it in the back. "It looks beautiful on you."

I examined myself in the pier glass. A grown-up stranger was staring back at me. I turned my head sideways. My neck was long and graceful, like that of a swan. *Yonah would think that I was pretty if he saw me now,* I said to myself.

"This necklace is so fine, more delicate than any I've seen before," I told Brianda.

"I want you to have it." Her wide smile slashed across her broad face. "Luis will tell you that you are beautiful when he sees you wearing it."

"I couldn't accept such a gift. You are too generous. Wear it yourself!"

Brianda sighed. "Such delicate jewelry wouldn't suit me. What was Father thinking when he bought it for me?" She pinched her fleshy chin and made a face. "My mother is right. I am too plump."

"You are not! Any girl would look lovely in such a beautiful necklace."

"I wouldn't. My neck is too fat." She scowled at her reflection in the mirror. "I shouldn't eat so many cakes. That stupid slave shouldn't have offered them to me."

"She had to. She was passing the tray around. How could she leave you out?" I couldn't help myself. "Why did you accuse her of dropping the cake? She did nothing wrong."

Brianda shrugged. "I was angry. Who cares? She is just a slave." She helped me undo the clasp at the back of the necklace. "You are lucky. Luis is so handsome. You must love him very much." She straightened the collar of her dress and sighed again. "I wish that Father would find me a husband just like Luis, but Father is too cheap. Mother says that he refuses to give me a dowry as generous as yours. She'll talk to him again when he comes home from the orchards, but it won't do any good," she said petulantly.

"Be careful what you wish for. Luis isn't . . ."

Mara appeared in the doorway. Her features were calm and composed. "Don Enrique has returned. He requests your presence downstairs, Doña Isabel."

I followed her out of the room. I knew better than to keep Papa waiting.

Mama sent Yussuf to the kitchen when we arrived home.

"The time has come to tell Isabel everything," Papa said. "Let's go to your chamber. We are less likely to be overheard there."

Papa locked the door behind us. He and Mama

looked so solemn that my heart began to drum uncontrollably. Mama and I sat down on the edge of her bed as Papa paced the length of the room. Abruptly, he stopped in front of me.

"Let's get it over with," he said. "Did you wonder, my daughter, why Fray Torquemada condescended to stop to talk to us today?"

"If you were more familiar with the world outside of our home, you would have heard that the Grand Inquisitor is not known for his friendliness," Mama added. "Did you wonder why he was curious about our family?"

I shook my head.

She clasped my hands in hers. "My darling, what we are about to tell you is difficult to believe – another secret that you must keep to yourself."

"Too many secrets, Mama . . ."

"We just want to protect you."

I cast down my eyes, for she always said that she could read my face like a book. I didn't want her to guess that I had told Yonah about our family's Jewish past. She wouldn't understand. Nor would Papa. They would be furious – they didn't know him like I did. They wouldn't believe that he would never betray us.

"Show the package to Isabel," Mama said. "That's the easiest way to explain."

Papa walked over to an ornately carved ebony bureau and pulled out the bottom drawer. He turned the drawer upside down, dumping a tangle of Mama's linens onto her bed. Then he pressed on the bottom left corner of the drawer with his fingers. Suddenly, the bottom of the drawer slid open, revealing a hidden compartment. There was an object in it, wrapped in white rags.

"The drawer has a false bottom," Papa explained. "You see that your mother keeps her linens in the top compartment. I'll show you what we have below them."

He took the package out and gently unwrapped it, uncovering a roll of parchment. He put it down on the bureau, unrolled the delicate page, and smoothed it down.

"Fortunately for us, your great-great-grandfather was an enlightened man," he said. "He taught both of his daughters to read and write. This is a letter written by Fray Torquemada's grandmother, her name was Sara, to your great-grandmother Miriam. It reveals that the two women were sisters. It proves, without doubt, that both of them were of the Jewish faith. Sara lived in Cordova after she married, while your great-grandmother dwelt here, in Toledo. Torquemada's grandmother wrote down in this letter the recipes for the dishes that their mother used to cook for the Jewish holiday of Passover. And here she wishes her sister a happy and healthy Passover."

I hardly knew what to say.

"How did you come by this letter, Papa?" I finally asked.

"I found it," Mama said. "About a year ago, I was looking for one of my linens when I accidentally pulled out the drawer too far. The drawer fell to the ground and the secret compartment popped open. The letter was in it. Your father's family has lived in this villa for generations. Who knows who hid it or how long it has been in the secret compartment."

"May I see it?"

"Come and look," Papa said.

Although the ink was faded, the markings made by a fine quill on the parchment were still easy to see. My heart filled with wonder as I read Doña Sara's words to her sister.

Papa rolled up the parchment and wrapped it in the white rags. He put it back into the secret compartment and gently pushed the false bottom of the drawer closed. Carefully, he slid the drawer back into the bureau and replaced Mama's linens.

"The Inquisition is quick to accuse New Christians of heresy, of disregarding the doctrines of the mother church," he said. "The Inquisitors are fanatic about *limpieza de sangre,* the purity of our blood. They say that our blood is tainted by the blood of our Jewish forefathers, and that the blood of Old Christians is pure."

"But Papa, if Fray Torquemada's grandmother was Jewish, wouldn't he be a New Christian, a Converso, just like us?"

"I told you that our daughter was clever," Mama said.

"You are perfectly right," my father said. "The Grand Inquisitor is a Converso but nobody knows. Or if they do, they are too frightened to speak of it. Nobody, except for us, knows about the existence of this letter, and that's the way it must remain – unless the unthinkable happens and we are accused of heresy. Do you understand?"

"I do, Papa."

"If we were imprisoned by the Inquisition and Torquemada found out about this letter, he would let us go."

"Because we are his relatives?"

"No, Isabel. He would free us if we threatened to expose his Converso background. The letter is our proof."

"Have you lost your senses, Enrique?" Mama asked.

"You don't threaten a man like the Grand Inquisitor. If we said anything about the letter to him, he would have us tortured until we 'confessed' that it was a forgery. He is so cruel that he can make anybody confess to anything. And then when they do confess, he burns them at the stake."

Papa shook his head. "You're wrong, Catarina." He turned back to me. "Don't listen to your mother. Torquemada wouldn't want people talking about this letter behind his back. They might believe what it says despite a 'confession' that states that it is a forgery. If we ever found ourselves in the clutches of the Inquisition, the letter would be our only weapon."

Mama's hands were clasped tightly in her lap. "Torquemada is without mercy. God forbid that we should ever find ourselves in such a terrible position."

Papa pulled a beautifully carved bench away from the wall and sat down facing me and Mama. He leaned so close to me that I could see every pore, every wrinkle in his face. "Forget for now that you ever saw this letter," he said. "You must not use it unless it is absolutely necessary. Unless it is a question of life and death. Do you understand?"

"I do."

"Promise me that you will never tell anybody about it."

"I swear, Papa. I won't tell."

Not even Yonah. It's safer for him not to know of its existence, I said to myself.

CHAPTER 6

THURSDAY, DECEMBER 15, 1491

"Where are we going?"

"Just follow me," Yonah said.

He led me down Potters' Alley, past vendors selling clay dishes of every type. Urns to hold wine competed for space with plates that would grace the tables of the residents of Toledo. He was walking so fast that I had to run to keep up with him. By the time we got to Tanners' Row, I begged him to slow down.

"Wait for me!"

"We're almost there." He stopped so that I could catch up.

We turned the corner to Bakers' Lane. The aroma of fresh bread made my mouth water. We passed the large building that housed the public ovens and stopped in front of a bakery. Yonah looked in both directions, but nobody in the street was paying attention to two Jewish boys out on an errand. He was in a homespun cloak with a pointed hood that Jews had to wear. I was dressed in a similar garment. Sofia had bought it for me at the market. Both Yonah and I had the badge of the Jews on our shoulders.

We slipped into the shop. It was small and dark. A table in the middle of the room was covered by loaves of bread of every shape and size. Wooden racks along the walls displayed more bread. Large bins full of bread dough were scattered all over the shop. Flour covered everything, including the grim face and clothing of the old man kneading dough in a corner. He threw us a glance.

Yonah's eyes darted around the shop. When he saw that we were alone with the man, he gave a sigh of relief. "How goes it, Pedro?" he asked.

The man grunted.

An old woman in tattered clothes came into the shop. The baker gave her an oily smile.

She picked up a small loaf from one of the racks on the wall. "I don't know how you can charge for such poor bread," she whined.

"You know that you really love my loaves, Mother," the baker said in a jolly voice.

She pressed a few coins into his palm and waddled

out of the bakery.

"Stupid, old witch," the baker murmured as he dropped the money into the greasy pouch hanging around his neck. "You're late," he said to Yonah. He nodded toward the floor. "The rest of them are already here." He walked over to the door leading to the street and blocked it with his bulk.

Yonah pushed a wooden chest away from the wall, revealing the outline of a trapdoor on the floor. He lifted the trapdoor and climbed into the opening. I knelt and peered into the darkness below. Yonah was at the bottom of a ladder attached to the underside of the shop's wooden floor.

"Come down," he whispered.

As I climbed down after him, I heard the trapdoor shut above my head and the scraping noise of the chest being dragged over it. I groped for the next rung with my foot.

It took a few minutes for my eyes to adjust to the darkness. A single lit taper flickered in the middle of a rough-hewn table in the center of the room. It cast flickers of light that danced over the faces of the people sitting around it. Most of them seemed to be near my age. A man with a long, white beard sat at the head of the table.

"Welcome, Yonah," he said. "Who do you bring

with you?" Even in the gloom, the red and white patch was bright against his cloak.

Yonah pulled the hood of my cloak off my head.

"Her name is Isabel, Rabbi. She is one of the anusim, the forced ones. We thought it would be safer if she disguised herself as a boy. She wants to know more about us."

I leaned close to his ear. "Why do you call me an anusim?"

"Because your family was forced to convert by the sword. They had to convert or die."

"Were you careful? Did anybody follow you?" a woman asked, her voice muffled by the hood of her cloak.

"We were cautious. Nobody was paying us any attention."

"I am Rabbi Abenbilla, child," said the man with the beard. "So you want to learn about the Jewish religion?"

"I do, Rabbi."

As soon as the words left my mouth, I knew that I was telling the truth. At first, I had agreed to accompany Yonah because I wanted to be with him. Now, despite my fears, I did want to know more.

"You've come to the right place. Welcome to our little group. We come together every fortnight to study Torah."

A pretty girl sitting next to the rabbi smiled at me warily. "My name is Judit. Here I am called Yehudit," she said. "I am an anusim."

A boy piped up across the table. "So am I! My name is Alberto."

"Time to get back to our studies," the rabbi said. "Who can tell us what happened to the Jewish people after they escaped from slavery in the land of the pharaohs?"

Alberto stood up and adjusted his fine silk collar. "Moses went up Mount Sinai – "

Suddenly heavy footsteps boomed overhead. Alberto fell silent. We could hear banging and loud men's voices, but we couldn't make out what they were saying. Rabbi Abenbilla snuffed out the candle. We sat in the thick darkness, afraid even to breathe. Over and over, I murmured the Hail Mary to myself. I was glad of Yonah's hand sneaking into mine.

After what seemed like hours but couldn't have been more than a few minutes, it was quiet again. The trapdoor lifted and Pedro's face appeared.

"You can come up now!"

When I reached the top of the ladder and came to stand with the others, I saw that Pedro was bent over, clutching his stomach. Blood ran down his face from a cut above his eyes, staining his clothes. The little bakery had been destroyed. The table that had held the freshly baked bread was on its side, its legs broken. The bread dough had been hurled against the walls and ceiling.

"What happened?" Rabbi Abenbilla asked, looking around at the shambles.

"The Inquisition was here," Pedro said in a hoarse whisper. "Three familiars came into the shop. They asked me if I sold bread to Jews. When I said that I did, they beat me with their clubs. After they had their fun with me, they took their clubs to my shop. May the bastards be cursed!" He spat on the floor. "They said that if I let Jews into my shop again, I would have to appear before the Inquisition."

Rabbi Abenbilla took a handful of coins out of his pocket and held them out to Pedro. "I am sorry we can't stay to help you clean up. It would be too dangerous. The money will help rebuild your shop. We will find somewhere else to meet."

The baker pushed aside the rabbi's hand. "I don't need your charity," he said gruffly. "I don't need to be paid to help you. You can come back here. Just be careful." He shook his hair out of his eyes. "Those bastards might return. Go now! It would be worse for all of us if they found you here."

———

As we made our way through the busy streets, I was glad of Yonah's arm under mine, guiding me. I took a deep breath and held my face up toward the sun. The world seemed a more vivid, a more colorful place than ever before. My body felt light, as if I could fly, without my heavy velvet clothes to weigh me down.

Yonah stopped when we arrived at the Bisagra Gate at the walls of Toledo.

"Look!" he whispered. Amid a noisy crowd, the town crier and a familiar in distinctive black clothing were nailing a proclamation to the gate.

"Attention, one and all!" shouted the town crier.

The familiar pulled out a rolled-up document from beneath his doublet. He undid it and began to read. "Citizens of Toledo! I speak to you on behalf of the holy Inquisition. I bring you this Edict of Grace at the behest of the Inquisitor General Fray Tomás de Torquemada. The Inquisition requires those of you who have fallen away from Christ to come forward out of your own volition and to confess your heresy in front of the holy Inquisition. Their excellencies have given you a term of grace of thirty days. If you admit your wrongdoings in front of the holy Inquisition in less than thirty days hence, you will be allowed to repent and you will be treated mercifully by their excellencies, the Inquisitors of Toledo. Only voluntary confession will save your souls from everlasting damnation and the long, just arm of the holy Inquisition."

When he paused to clear his throat, excited chatter erupted in the crowd. He held up his hand for silence before nudging the town crier in the ribs with his elbow.

The town crier turned to the proclamation on the gate and began to read. "It is your duty to report the transgressions of false Christians to the holy Inquisition. You will know that your neighbor is a heretic if he is a Christian who lights candles on Friday nights before sunset. You will know that your neighbor is a heretic if he bathes before the Jewish Sabbath. You will know that your neighbor is a heretic if he is a Christian who wears clean clothes and does not light a fire in his abode on the Jewish Sabbath. You will know that your neighbor is a heretic if he is a Christian who refuses to eat pork. You will know that your neighbor is a heretic if he is a Christian who blesses his children without making the sign of the cross. You will know that your neighbor is a heretic if he is a Christian who celebrates the Jewish festival of the unleavened bread. It is your duty as good Christians to report to the holy office heresy committed by your family, by your friends, and by your neighbors."

After he finished reading the proclamation, the

familiar grabbed his horse's bridle and swung himself into the saddle.

A man pushed his way to the front of the listeners. "Master," he asked, "can you tell us if – "

"I will tell you nothing more!" the familiar cried.

"Bastards!" Yonah muttered.

The familiar threw a coin at the boy who was holding his horse and then he was gone. The town crier left hot on his heels. The boy scrabbled around in the dust, trying to find the money.

"Let's go home! I want to tell my mama and my papa about this."

"How can you? They would ask where you heard it. You'll have to come up with a good excuse."

"I'll think of something."

We had just passed through the city gates when the clop-clop of galloping horsemen made us scurry to the side of the road. Everything happened so fast that the riders had already reached us by the time I realized that Luis was leading the pack. Before I could turn away, I felt his eyes on my face. Then he was gone.

I tugged at Yonah's sleeve. "That was Luis! He saw me!"

"How do you know?"

"He looked straight at me! He must have recognized me."

"How could he?" Yonah squeezed my hand. "Don't worry. All he saw was a Jewish boy – not the pampered Doña Isabel."

I tried to tell myself that he was right, but the memory of Luis's cold eyes horrified me. We melted into the crowd around us in case Luis decided to return. He did not come back.

I snuck upstairs to my room without anyone seeing me. Sofia helped me change. I was rushing so much that I was still out of breath when I went to look for Mama. She was in the courtyard, walking. She kissed me on the forehead.

"Luis is coming for supper tonight," she said.

"Again?" I asked, stepping in line with her stroll.

A tightening of her lips was the only sign that she had heard me. "Change into another dress," she continued.

I lifted the green skirt of the gown I was wearing. "What's wrong with my clothes?"

"Nothing. Your dress is pretty enough, but you have nicer ones." She cocked her head. "Let me see . . . wear your yellow gown, the one embroidered with silver threads. It's important that you look your best tonight."

She quickened her pace and walked toward the entrance to the house, leaving me behind.

I called after her. "Oh, Mama! You know how I feel about – "

She turned around and stopped. "No time for that now!" she said with an impatient wave.

I did not dare to disobey her.

Sofia tamed my curls with a snood. I changed into one of my most elegant dresses. My skirts whispered along the stone floor in a dignified manner as I walked. Only the tips of my jeweled slippers were visible. I could not have looked more different from the grimy Jewish boy I'd pretended to be at the city gates. I kept my eyes cast down modestly as I made my way toward the ornate trestle table in the middle of the dining hall. Papa and Luis rose from their seats.

Mama looked as handsome as ever in red silk. "You are late, daughter," she said.

The doors to the hall burst open. Two servants entered, carrying a suckling pig on a large silver tray. A large apple was in the pig's mouth, and the animal was surrounded by a mountain of cabbage and other vegetables from our garden. I glanced at Mama. This was the first time that I had seen pork served in our home.

She did not meet my gaze, her hand fluttering at her throat. I sat down beside her, across the table from Luis. He nodded in my direction but did not greet me.

"So much food for the three of us. The servants must be hungry!" Papa laughed.

He sliced off a large piece of pork and put it on Luis's plate. He cut another slice and started to pass it to Mama.

She pushed away his hand. "My stomach is queasy. I better not eat anything tonight – although there is nothing I like more than pork roasted in a pit!"

"You must have some of this delicious meat." Papa's voice was steely. "It'll settle your stomach." He put the meat on Mama's plate and added some cabbage. Then it was my turn before he helped himself to the pork.

My father ate calmly, his face determined. Mama cut her meat into small pieces. I noticed that she ate only the cabbage, that not a single mouthful of the pork touched her lips. She toyed with her food, covering the meat with the rest of her cabbage. I chewed and chewed, but the unfamiliar taste made me nauseous. I shot a quick glance at Luis. He was intent on tearing away at his meat greedily with his hands, grease shining on his chin.

Suddenly, he looked up. My expression must have revealed my disgust.

"You don't approve of my appetite, my lady? Or

perhaps you don't like pork?" His voice was harsh.

I realized that it would be foolish and dangerous to antagonize him. I smiled flirtatiously. "Pork is my favorite dish. I am glad that you are enjoying your food. A man must eat to remain strong!"

He laughed. I balled my fists to prevent myself from hitting him.

"Tell me, Isabel, how was your day? What did you do today?" Luis's eyes burrowed into my face.

I forced myself to speak in a languid tone. "I must confess that I was lazy today. I walked in the rose garden. You should come with me sometimes, Luis," I forced myself to say.

He grunted in reply.

"After my walk, I worked at my loom. I saw Father Juan for my weekly catechism lessons. Then I rested in my room for a while." I leaned toward him. "What about you, my lord? How did you spend your day?"

Mama was staring at me in surprise. She was used to curt replies whenever Luis addressed me.

"I went with friends to the bullfight."

I picked up my fan and hid behind it. "Was it to your liking?"

"Excellent. The matador gored the bull." He laughed at the poor animal's cruel fate and turned his attention back to his meal.

———

"Sofia, come and help me get ready for bed!" I called down the stairs.

She rushed into my bedchamber, her face flushed, her skirts askew.

"What's the matter with you?"

"I am glad that you called me, young mistress. It gave me the excuse to get away from that Habib!"

"Habib?"

"Don Luis's new servant. You would think that he had more hands than an octopus." She straightened her skirts. "You can be sure that I boxed his ears!" She came closer. "Be careful, mistress," she whispered. "Habib was asking about you. He wanted to know where you had gone today."

Were secretiveness and deceit another two of Luis's virtues? He had not revealed his suspicions to me at dinner tonight. "What did you say to Habib?"

She drew herself up to her full height. "Young mistress, you know that I would never betray you. I told him exactly what you told me to say if anyone asked – that you were resting in your chamber most of the afternoon." She shook her head. "I still don't think you should be gallivanting about with that Jewish boy, especially without a chaperone, even if the Jews are not as bad as I thought before. They seemed no different from other folks when I went to their Juderia."

I patted her hand. "Thank you, Sofia. I know how much I can rely on you." I could see by the smile playing on her lips that my compliment pleased her.

I tossed and turned in my bed for hours that night, my fears keeping sleep away. Had Luis recognized me at the gate to the city? If he did, why didn't he say so?

Chapter 7

It was the week before Christmas and the house was filled with the aromas of cooking. I knew that an elaborate feast would be waiting for us when we returned from mass. Tia Juana and Brianda would be joining us. I was glad of their company, for our house seemed so empty. Two days ago, Papa had left us for the royal court in Granada. The armies of Queen Isabella and King Ferdinand were waging war against the Moors. Their majesties were embarked upon the re-conquest of the Kingdom of Granada and of the Alhambra Palace, the Moorish stronghold. The armies of the caliphs had occupied Granada many years ago, but our queen and king were determined to win it back for Christendom. I missed Papa and prayed every day for his safe return.

There was another absence – and I was glad of it. Luis had left Toledo to spend the holidays on his family's estate in the kingdom of Aragon. I felt safe for the first time since I met him. Mama shared my feelings.

"It'll be a pleasure not to have to serve pork, as we always do when he comes for dinner," she said.

The air was fresh and cool when Mama and I walked to the cathedral, the Church of Santo Tome. Yussuf led the way, making way for us through the streets. We found Tia Juana and Brianda waiting at the church, in the midst of an excited crowd. Their manservant was with them, making sure that nobody jostled them.

"What's happening here?" Mama asked.

"Three heretics are trying to enter the house of our Lord," Tia Juana said. "The crowd won't let them go inside."

"Perhaps we should go home," Mama suggested. "I don't think it's safe here."

"I don't want to miss mass! It's Christmas next week."

Mama slapped her forehead with her palm. "You are right, Juana. I forgot for a moment. Let's wait a little longer and see what happens."

I was standing close enough to hear the little sigh that had escaped her. "You may leave us, Yussuf," Mama said. "Ahmed will see us home safely."

Tia Juana's burly slave nodded his head.

"There are so many people here, Doña Catarina," Yussuf protested.

"Don't worry. We will wait beside the entrance until everybody has gone inside."

The Moor reluctantly bid us good-bye and left.

The people around us began to jeer when the three young men in the sambenitos tried to fight their way through the mob, only to be pushed back, again and again. One of them fell, but his friends saved him from being trampled by quickly pulling him to his feet. The boy turned around and – for the first time – I saw his face. It was Alberto from Yonah's Torah class in the basement of the bakery. His nose was bleeding and one of his eyes was starting to swell shut. His elegant clothes were in tatters. His eyes widened when he saw me, but he turned his head away. I felt certain that he had recognized me.

I took a step toward him, but Mama pulled me back. She was right to do so. What could I do against the anger of so many people? There was no way I could help Alberto.

"These boys should go home," I told Mama. "This crowd will never let them into the church."

"They can't go home," Mama said in an expressionless voice. "The Inquisition ordered them to confess their sins publicly in church every Sunday. They must listen to Father Juan's sermons in order to learn the teachings of our Lord. If they don't follow the rulings of the Inquisition, they will be punished."

"The holy office should have ordered them to be burned at the stake! They are Marranos who commit heresy." Tia Juana spat on the ground. I was shocked not only because of her crude behavior, but because I didn't recognize the aunt I knew, always ready for jollity, always full of compliments. "Look at what they are doing." She pointed her fan at the desperate young men.

Alberto had torn off his sambenito and was twirling it over his head. The crowd parted in horror, leaving an open path to the church.

"Go away! Don't touch us with that sambenito! Keep it away from us!" they cried.

Alberto kept twirling it around and around. He was grinning as he and the other penitents rushed into the church. The people surrounding them streamed in after them, careful to keep their distance. We were the last to enter. The carved wooden pews at the front, where we always sat, were waiting for us. The boys knelt in front of the altar, loudly confessing their sins.

"Repent!" cried a fat senora beside me.

"Give yourself up to Christ or you won't be saved,"

Father Juan said to them as he came to stand at the pulpit.

He began his sermon. I tried to pay attention, but my eyes became heavier and heavier. They flew open when I felt Brianda's elbow in my side.

"Thank you!" I whispered.

I looked around to keep awake. The church's walls were festooned with the sambenitos of the heretics who had been burned alive at the stake during different autos-de-fé.

"So many sambenitos," I whispered to Mama. "They should take them off the wall."

She rolled her eyes. "They are supposed to be reminders to the families of the condemned heretics. They are warnings to them not to follow in the footsteps of their relatives," she whispered. "They are a warning to us all."

Her words filled me with fear.

The sermon was finally over. Organ music filled the church, entering my soul. The smell of incense was pungent and familiar. When it was my turn to kneel before Father Juan to receive the sacraments, the wine tasted sour in my mouth and the host was bitter. I thought that my heart would break.

———

Christmas was lonely without Papa. Mama and I spent our time wondering what he was doing.

A week later, Luis was back in Toledo. He didn't waste time calling on us. He cornered me in the sitting room.

"Did you miss me?" he asked, running a finger down my arm.

"Of course, my lord."

I stood up and tried to pass him, but he grabbed my wrist and pulled me close. Although I pushed him away, he was much stronger than I.

"Let me go!"

"Aren't you going to welcome me home?" He lowered his head to kiss me and his sour breath made my stomach turn.

"My lord, you forget yourself." I stared over his shoulder. "Mama, I am so glad that you are here!"

He jumped back and dropped my hand. I picked up my skirts and ran out the door.

"You'll regret this!" he called after me.

CHAPTER 8

MONDAY, APRIL 2, 1492

The sun was low in the sky when I followed Yonah through the El Cambron Gate leading into the Juderia. We wore long cloaks with the red and white badges on them. Both of us were dressed in white boys' garments underneath. Again, I hid my hair under the pointed hood.

The shutters were closed tight over the shop windows, and the narrow streets of the Juderia were almost empty. We crossed in front of the El Transito Synagogue. The sound of praying wafted out through its open door. We turned down a street of narrow two-storey buildings, some of which had balconies decorated with six-pointed stars outlined in mosaic. The delicious odor of cooking food came through the windows we passed.

"People are at home, preparing for the first seder," Yonah said.

He stopped in front of a narrow house at the end of the street. When he rang the bell, the door was immediately opened by a small woman swathed from head to toe in voluminous clothing. Her plump face was wreathed in smiles.

"Come in," she said, pulling us inside.

I pulled off the hood of my cloak and curtsied.

"Good evening, Rebbetzin Abenbilla. It's so kind of you to invite me and Isabel to your home for Pesach," Yonah said.

The Rabbi's wife looked around the hall in an exaggerated manner. "I don't see an Isabel here, but both you and your friend Yaacov are welcome to join us to remember the exodus of our people from slavery in Egypt." She walked over to the window. "The sun is setting! Follow me."

She led us into a small chamber full of people. A rough-hewn table was covered by an embroidered white cloth and set with pretty pottery dishes. Seven unlit candles stood on the table.

Rabbi Abenbilla sat at the head of the table. Seated to his left was his son Shmuel, who couldn't have been more than ten years of age. I recognized the others as the anusim from our study group. Everybody was dressed in white.

"Hello, Isabel," said a familiar voice behind me.

It was Yehudit. I hugged her. Alberto followed her in, the hated sambenito flung over his arm. He dropped it onto the back of a chair.

"I was afraid that I wouldn't get here before the sun set. My mother asked me to run errands, and I couldn't get away earlier," Yehudit said.

"I had to tell my mama that I was visiting my friend Brianda and that Sofia, my slave, was chaperoning me."

The rabbi's wife invited us to sit down and we crowded around the table.

She carried in from the kitchen the Passover plate of traditional foods with great ceremony and set it down on the table in front of her husband. Then she lit the seven candles and her husband began reading the Passover service from a beautiful illustrated Haggadah that tells the story of Passover. He stroked the colorful pages with gentle fingers.

We named the plagues by which God forced Pharaoh to allow his Jewish slaves to leave Egypt. We broke the matzo in its center and dipped it twice into wine. Every person around the seder table whipped the wrist of his neighbor with the stems of green onions while we sang "Dayenu," a song that gives thanks to God for leading the Jewish people out of slavery in Egypt. The sound made by the onion stems reminded us of the whipping our ancestors received in Egypt at Pharaoh's cruel hands. Yonah was chosen to represent Pharaoh and he walked around the table wearing a crown of clay to witness the whipping of his "slaves."

Rabbi Abenbilla tied the *afikomen,* a piece of broken matzo, into a large napkin and gave it to young Smuel. The boy slung the napkin over his shoulder and left the room. When he knocked on the door, requesting entry, the rabbi addressed him.

"From where do you come?"

"I come from Egypt," Shmuel said.

"Where are you going?" the rabbi asked.

"To Jerusalem."

"What are you taking with you?" asked his father.

Smuel pointed to the matzo in his napkin.

Then all of us began to chant. "Why is this night different from all other nights?"

I looked around the table. The flickering candlelight lit the smiles on the faces of my new friends. Yonah's hand slipped into mine. I closed my eyes. For a moment, the smell of incense filled my nostrils and a memory of the crown of thorns on the head of Christ made my heart ache.

"Welcome home," Yonah whispered.

My eyes flew open. I shook my head to chase away the ghosts, and I squeezed his fingers.

It took me a moment to realize that Yehudit was speaking to me from my other side. "Let's help Rebbetzin Abenbilla."

Yehudit and I carried trays piled high with different kinds of delicacies to the table until there was no more room for anything else. I tasted, for the first time, a dish of *huevos haminados,* brown eggs cooked in the oven for a whole day over low heat. They were delicious. The Rebbetzin told me that they were eaten every Passover. Next came roasted lamb, baked fish with vegetables and rice, and, finally, almond cakes. Oranges, bananas, and pomegranates filled a bowl.

Yonah and I did not dare to stay until the end of the seder. I didn't want to be home late and have my mother start asking questions.

Sofia was waiting for us at the city gate.

"You were gone so long!" she cried. "Doña Catarina wanted to know where you were."

"What did you tell her?"

"That I went with you to Doña Brianda's house. I said that they invited you for supper."

"Did Mama believe you?"

She nodded. "She sent me to bring you home. We must hurry!"

I bid Yonah good-bye and he set out for his home in the *Aljama,* the Juderia. I followed Sofia through the city gates to the countryside, toward our estate.

Luck was on my side. Mama was in the kitchen berating one of the maids when I arrived home. Sofia and I snuck up to my room, climbing the back staircase the servants used. She helped me change into a gown and dressed my hair before I went downstairs.

My mother scolded me for being late.

"No guest should outstay her welcome," she said. "Juana is much too polite to ask you to go home. She'll think that I didn't teach you good manners."

"I am sorry, Mama. It won't happen again," I said meekly.

CHAPTER 9

SATURDAY, APRIL 28, 1492

The sun shining through the wooden shutters woke me up. Half asleep, I pulled the covers over my head until I suddenly remembered what day it was. I bolted up. It was my birthday! I was turning fifteen today, no longer a child. Old enough to marry. I pushed the thought out of my mind determinedly. I didn't want to think about Luis. Not today. I wanted to enjoy my birthday.

Papa had finally come home. He had been gone for over four months to help the queen and the king in the Reconquista of the Kingdom of Granada, the last stronghold of the Moors in Christian Spain. Mama and I had counted the days until his return. How we had worried about him! To our great delight, he had returned last night from their majesties' court. He had been muddy and exhausted but not too tired to engulf

Mama in a hug and to spin me around the room.

After he had washed, he called for wine to be brought to us in the courtyard. He was bursting with wonderful news. On the second day of January of our Lord in 1492, he had ridden with the armies of Queen Isabella and King Ferdinand into the Alhambra Palace in the Kingdom of Granada. The fortress palace was now occupied by their Catholic majesties and their royal court. The Spanish army had been victorious over the Moors.

Though it was very late, Papa had described the palace to us. "I give you my oath that I will take you both to the Alhambra some day. It is paradise on earth. It is different from anything that you could possibly imagine."

He described halls with walls of tiles painted vivid blue, red, and golden yellow, and he spoke of high, high arches and ceilings that looked like the honeycombs of bees. He talked of cool courtyards and fountains with stone lions that spouted water.

"The most amazing of all," he said, "are the gardens – so lush, so beautiful, so full of birdsong. The gardens are so vast that you can lose yourself in them. There are roses, oranges, myrtles, and reflecting pools of utter stillness. My soul felt at peace whenever I rested beside one of them."

He described how Boabdil, caliph of the Moors, had handed the keys to the palace to their Catholic majesties on a bent knee. The winter sun gleamed on Queen Isabel's crown of eagles. Tears were running down Boabdil's face as he rode away with his defeated army.

Papa stayed in bed most of the day. We hushed the servants and spoke as quietly as we could until he woke refreshed and energetic and calling to his Moor to bring him warm ale.

There was to be a feast to celebrate both Papa's return and my birthday. Brianda and her family were invited. They would be spending the night with us because the gates to Toledo would be locked by the time the celebration ended. Unfortunately, Luis would be there, too. It couldn't be helped.

I had arranged to meet Yonah under our orange tree after my birthday celebration. How I wished that he could be with my family! However, I knew that Mama and Papa would never allow our friendship. All I could do was hug my secret to my heart and count the minutes until I saw him again.

Mama was in the kitchen giving instructions to Sofia and to the other servants. She had asked the cook to bake almond tarts, like the ones we had eaten at Tia Juana's house.

"I am certain that you can bake cakes that are more delicious than those from Doña Juana's kitchen," she wheedled. "Doña Juana always claims that her household is better run than mine, that her cook is more skilled than you. We'll show her how wrong she is!"

The cook bobbed a curtsy. "My lady, if I bake the almond tarts, I won't have time to go to Farmers' Alley. We need dates and pistachios and apples from the farmers' orchards."

"Send one of the scullery maids," Mama said.

"Sofia and the other girls are preparing the chambers upstairs for our guests. There is nobody to send except Yussuf. He has never gone to the market by himself. He won't know what to buy."

"I'll go with Yussuf, Mama. I'll help him pick good fruit."

She shook her head. "I don't like the idea of you on the street with only the Moor for protection. I'll go, although I have so much to do."

"I can go, Mama. I'll be safe with Yussuf."

Sofia appeared in the doorway. "Doña Catarina, could you please come upstairs? Those stupid girls won't listen to me!"

Mama looked at me and then at Sofia.

"It won't take me long to buy what we need," I promised in my most reassuring tone.

There was a loud bang over our heads.

Mama threw her hands up. "All right, but you must be back in an hour or I'll come looking for you."

She hurried out of the kitchen, followed by Sofia.

"We'll save time if we cross the Plaza de Zocodover," Yussuf said.

I followed him to the square. When we turned the corner, we came to a sudden stop. The plaza was filled with people. Two stands had been built at the back of the square. One was occupied by clergy and nobility in rich garments, the other by dirty wretches in sambenitos. Linking the two stands was an altar draped in black, with a cross attached to it. I barely noticed the stands. My eyes were riveted on a pyre in the middle of the square. Men and women were tied to stakes and being burned alive. It was an auto-de-fé, an act of faith, the public burning of heretics convicted by the Inquisition. I had never seen one before. I closed my eyes, but when I opened them again, I saw the same dreadful sight. Screams of agony filled the air. A lout, carrying a burning staff, ran up to one of the victims and lit the wretched man's beard on fire. The crowd roared. *How can they be so cruel?* I wondered. I hugged myself tightly.

Yussuf pulled on my sleeve. "Mistress, we must go!"

I barely heard him. "People are being burned alive!"

The stench of roasting flesh made me gag and I vomited. The Moor put his mighty arm around my shoulder and dragged me out of the plaza. He sat me down on the ground, under the shade of a tree. He wiped my face with the sleeve of his robe. He fanned me with his hands until the color returned to my cheeks.

"I am so sorry, young mistress." He hung his head. "You shouldn't have seen that. I didn't know that an auto-de-fé was being held in the plaza today." He beat his chest with his fists and moaned. "Ay! Ay! What have I done? My lady will never forgive me. The master will sell me to the galleys when he finds out what you've witnessed. I'll never see my wife and son again! Don Enrique, may Allah bless his name, frees all of us slaves after we serve him loyally for ten years. I will look for my family as soon as I become a free man. If I am sent to the galleys, they'll be forever lost to me!"

He looked so miserable that my heart filled with pity. "Don't worry. My parents won't blame you. I'll make sure that they don't. I'll tell them that it wasn't your fault. You aren't the only one who didn't know about the auto-de-fé. Mama couldn't have known either or she would never have agreed to my leaving the house with you." I held out my hand and he helped me up. "Let's go and buy the fruit. I want to go home."

Mama took one look at my face and demanded to know what had happened.

I told her about the living nightmare we had witnessed. "Those poor people. Suffering so terribly! How can the Inquisition be so cruel as to burn them alive?" Even thinking about it made me feel queasy.

Mama patted my hand. "Hush!" she said. "You mustn't criticize the Inquisition! Somebody might overhear you."

"It wasn't Yussuf's fault that we went to the plaza. He didn't know that an auto-de-fé was being held there."

She sat down heavily. "Don't worry about the Moor. I don't blame him. I blame myself. I forgot all about the auto in the excitement of your father's homecoming." She fanned herself thoughtfully for a moment. "We wanted to spare you such sights and we were able to do so up to now because most autos are outside the city. Perhaps it's good that you saw one and finally know what's happening. The Inquisition has eyes and ears everywhere. You can't trust anyone. No one is safe. Your best friend today might turn out to be your worst enemy tomorrow."

The shock was catching up with me. I felt myself sway.

"Isabel, you've been badly shaken. Go to your room and rest," Mama said.

The table was set with heavy silver dishes that held delicacies of every kind. In the place of honor, in the center of the table, the little golden bird in its silver cage sang its silent song. We ate and ate and drank and drank until we couldn't have eaten another morsel or drunk another drop of wine. Finally, it was time for me to receive my presents.

Brianda placed a package wrapped in fine white cloth in my hands. It contained the same delicate necklace that I had admired on our last visit.

"I can't accept this." I pushed it into her hands. "This is too fine a gift. I told you before."

"It looks much better on you than on me. Please take it." She handed it back to me.

"It's yours, little one," Tia Juana said, smiling. "Her father will buy her another necklace, one she likes better."

"Even nicer than this one," Diego de Alvarez said, smiling fondly at his daughter.

Brianda jumped up from her seat and put it around my neck. I ran my fingers over it. It was light as a feather against my skin.

"You look beautiful in it," Brianda said.

Both Mama and Tia Juana nodded their approval.

Next, it was Luis's turn. He held out a velvet pouch. In it was a gold bracelet studded with garish green stones as big as pebbles. He slipped it onto my wrist. It was so heavy that I felt I couldn't lift my arm. *This is how the shackles of a galley slave must feel,* I said to myself. I lowered my eyes so that he wouldn't guess my thoughts.

"Thank you," I mumbled.

"This magnificent bracelet shows Luis's regard for you," Papa said firmly. "You must tell him how much you like it."

Mama kept her gaze on her hands, which were clenched together in her lap so tightly that her knuckles were white.

"Tell Luis how much you like the bracelet," Papa repeated.

I looked up and forced myself to smile. "It's a beautiful bracelet . . . very . . . regal!"

He nodded. "As it should be. Nothing but the best for my betrothed, soon to be my bride. May I reap my reward?"

I looked at Papa pleadingly. He suddenly became absorbed in his food. Mama was still as a statue. Luis leaned closer. Without waiting for my reply, he kissed me. I turned my head and his lips missed my mouth, landing on my cheek. His lips were cold against my face. Suddenly, I remembered the baby lizard wriggling under his heel in the rose garden and I shuddered. He drew back, his eyes glistening his fury.

Papa broke the awkward silence with a brisk clap of his hands. A tall, turbaned Moor entered the room. It was the slave who had accompanied Papa home from Granada. He was carrying a large package in his arms, and a square of crimson silk was draped on top. He put the package on the table in front of me, bowed, and backed out of the room.

"Remove the kerchief," Papa said.

I pulled it off and found myself staring at a trembling, little lark with brown feathers.

"I remembered how much you liked this golden bird," Papa said, pointing to Yonah's masterpiece. "I bought you a live one!"

"Your father carried the little creature home all the way from Granada," Mama added.

"It comes from the gardens of the Alhambra, from paradise on earth," Papa said. "May your life be as pleasant as if you were living in paradise."

I threw my arms around his neck. "Oh, Papa. Thank you! My own songbird. I love it!"

I put my finger through the bars of the cage and smoothed down the tiny bird's feathers.

"Poor little creature," I said softly, "you may live in a cage, away from your home, and you may be forced to sing your songs all alone, but you will be happy with me for I will take good care of you."

The bird ruffled its feathers and burst into a song of such sweetness that I thought my heart would melt.

"What will you call it?" Mama asked.

I thought long and hard until its name became clear in my mind. "Its name is Anusim. It means 'the forced one.'"

Papa gave me a sharp look.

"That's a silly name for a bird," Brianda said.

"I heard it from one of the servants . . . I can't remember which one." I kept my voice casual. "The name suits the bird. It's forced to live in a cage and to sing its songs in captivity." I stroked its feathers again. "Don't worry, little one. I'll take good care of you."

The night was as dark as ink. I could barely see farther than the tip of my nose. I dragged my hand along the side of the house as I made my way to the orange tree.

Yonah was waiting.

"I hoped that you could come."

"The feast lasted forever. Afterward, Brianda wanted to talk. I had to wait until she fell asleep." I sat down on the grass beside him. "How I wish that you could have been with us tonight."

"I will be some day. And you will meet my father." His tone was so sure.

"You believe that?"

"With all my heart. We must be patient."

He took my hand and I lowered my head onto his shoulder.

"You'll never guess what a wonderful present Papa gave me. He brought me a songbird all the way from the Alhambra. It is so beautiful and its voice is so sweet. Papa says that he bought it for me because he remembered how much I love the golden bird you made for me."

"My father made it. I just helped."

"Don't be modest. The two of you made it together." I squeezed his hand. "I named the songbird Anusim because it is forced to live in a cage and sing its songs in captivity."

Yonah drew closer. "Let it go, Isabel. Let it be free."

"I can't! What would Papa say?"

"Tell him that you forgot to close the door of the cage and the bird flew away."

"A falcon might capture it and devour it. I am afraid to free it." I began to cry. "Why can't you be happy for me? I love to hear it sing."

I pressed his hand against my cheek and felt his fingers wiping away my tears.

"Don't cry, Isabel. Your tears break my heart."

The sweetness of his breath caressed my face.

"I have a gift for you, too," he said.

For a moment, the moon appeared and I was able to see what he had given me. It was a small silver cup with intricate designs imprinted onto its surface.

"It's a kiddush cup. We use it to hold the wine we drink to welcome the Sabbath," Yonah explained.

"It's beautiful!"

"I made it."

Suddenly, the bushes rustled nearby.

Yonah got to his feet. "Who is there?" he called out.

There was no answer.

He pulled me up from the grass. "Go back to the house, Isabel! I'll come with you."

"No! It's too risky."

He put his arm around my shoulders and hurried me along the wall to a side door. We stopped there. For a fleeting moment I thought that I felt his lips brush my hair, but it was so dark that I couldn't be sure.

"Go!" he whispered. "Go back to your bed."

"I won't leave you."

"You must."

"How will you get back into Toledo?"

"I won't. At least not until the morning. I'll catch some rest by the city gate. I won't be the only one."

I grabbed his arm. "When will I see you again?"

"I'll send you a message."

Then he was gone.

The house was silent as I crept up to my room, clutching the kiddush cup in my hand. *The noise in the bushes must have been an animal, most likely a badger,* I told myself. There was no one about, but candlelight was streaming out from beneath Mama's chamber. I heard the soft murmur of voices. I slowed to listen but thought better of stopping. If there was something important to know, Mama and Papa would tell me.

I closed the door of my room quietly. I held up the kiddush cup in the near-darkness. I turned it around and around to admire the beautiful engravings on it. Where to hide it? I decided to put it into the drawer in my armoire where I kept my petticoats. I was sure that it would be safe because nobody except for Sofia ever looked there. I slipped it among my petticoats in the half-open drawer, careful to smooth down the fine material on top of it.

I peeked at the bird asleep in its cage and climbed into bed. I tossed and turned, all kinds of thoughts crowding my head. What could my parents have been talking about? Did they have more secrets that I didn't know about? I tried to lie still to allow the cricket song outside my window to lull me to sleep, but sleep didn't come. I gave up and made my way down the quiet corridor to Mama's chamber.

I could still see the sliver of candlelight below the door. And their voices continued to whisper their secrets. I knocked softly.

I heard Mama gasp. "Did you hear a noise outside?"

Papa laughed. "Catarina, you are allowing your imagination to rule your common sense. It's probably Isabel." He opened the door for me. Mama was sitting on the side of her bed and there was a chair facing her, where Papa must have been sitting.

"I can't sleep, Papa."

Mama called me to her. "Lie down here, dear." She stood up and pulled the silk covers back. I slid into her bed and pulled the covers to my chin. She sat down at the foot of the bed, like she used to do when I was a little girl before telling me bedtime stories. I closed my eyes, feeling suddenly childlike and safe. I must have dozed off for a moment, but soon I woke up and listened to my parents' familiar voices again. I kept my eyes closed so they wouldn't send me back to my room.

"You're right, Enrique, but this news is so incredible that I am full of fear. Who would have ever imagined that their majesties are planning to expel the Jews from Sefarad?"

Expel the Jews? Yonah gone? I wanted to cry out, but I knew that my parents would send me back to my bed if they knew I was listening, so I squeezed my eyes shut.

"Why would the queen and the king treat the Jews so cruelly?" Mama asked. "The Jews of Sefarad have served the royal couple loyally – as did their parents and their parents before them. Don't Isabel and Ferdinand realize what the Jews have done for them?"

"They must realize it. The Jews loaned them the money that helped them reconquer Spain. Now Isabel and Ferdinand have succeeded, and they don't need the Jews' money."

"How did you hear this incredible news? Expelling all the Jews from the kingdom – it's unbelievable!"

"Let me tell you what happened," Papa answered. "I went to the throne room to bid their majesties goodbye the day before I was to come home. Of course I had heard rumors, but I didn't believe them for a moment."

"What rumors?"

"That the queen and the king signed an Edict of Expulsion that orders the Jews to leave Spain by the last day of July. And anybody who made this news public, who revealed it before it was announced, especially to the Jews themselves, would be put to death. As I said, I didn't believe a word of it at the time. The court is always full of false rumors."

"What made you change your mind?" I could hear the sound of wine being poured into a goblet.

"I'll never forget what I saw, what I heard." Papa sighed. "I went to the throne room of the Alhambra. Their majesties were seated on their jeweled thrones under an alabaster latticed window. I was about to approach them when the entrance to the hall opened and the Jewish courtiers Isaac Abravanel, their majesties' chief financial advisor, and old Rabbi Abraham Seneor, the judge of the Jews of Spain and the chief treasurer of the crown, were announced. I am certain that I must have told you before that Abravanel is their majesties' most faithful servant."

"Yes, you did say how loyal he was to Isabel and Ferdinand, how he used his own wealth to finance the Reconquista."

"Not only that. He had recently negotiated with Christopher Columbus on their majesties' behalf. Who knows what riches Columbus will bring to the kingdom when his ships sail? Rabbi Seneor is no less a friend to the royal couple than Abravanel. He was instrumental in arranging their marriage many years ago. He remained steadfast and loyal during the dark days of the civil war. He is the head of the hermandad, the police. When the queen and the king saw their old friends approaching, they smiled."

"Smiled? How could they smile when they already sealed the fate of these men, when they exiled them from their homes?"

I could feel Mama's anger.

Papa cleared his throat. "Royalty is different from the rest of us. Let me tell you what happened next. The two courtiers fell to their knees in front of the monarchs. The queen leaned forward as if to help Seneor stand up. The old man must be at least eighty years of age."

Papa paused.

"The two men reminded Isabel and Ferdinand of the loyalty of their Jewish subjects to the crown over many generations, and of their own devotion to the queen and the king, and of their love for their kingdom. They begged the monarchs to cancel the Edict of

Expulsion. They advised Isabel and Ferdinand to tax the Jews even more than they are already taxed, instead of expelling them from Sefarad."

"Why would they say that?" Mama asked.

"The crown would gain the Jews' property if they expelled them from the kingdom. Abravanel and Seneor were suggesting another way for the crown to get hold of Jewish money."

"Will their majesties' greed never be satisfied?"

"Hush now, and listen to what happened next," Papa said. "Abravanel made a most extraordinary suggestion. He offered the king and the queen thirty thousand gold ducats if they allowed the Jews to stay in their homes."

"His own fortune? What a noble man."

"Yes, Isaac Abravanel is a true cavalier. He is a man of principle."

There was a long moment of silence, then Mama's voice. "Isabel, are you awake?"

I knew there was no use in trying to pretend any longer, and certainly no use in trying to fall asleep. Mama adjusted the pillows so I could sit up and she poured a goblet of wine for me.

Papa continued his story. "As soon as Abravanel made his offer, the queen sat up straighter on her throne. A nasty little smile appeared upon the king's lips. 'Thirty thousand gold ducats you are offering us, Don Isaac?' he asked. 'In that case, we must reconsider . . . ' At that very moment, a side door opened and Tomás de Torquemada burst into the throne room. He was trembling like the leaves of a fig tree in a storm and waving a crucifix."

Papa took a sip of his wine and went on. "'Behold the crucified Christ whom Judas Iscariot sold for thirty pieces of silver!' Torquemada cried. 'Your majesties are about to sell him again for thirty thousand pieces of gold. You shall have to answer to God!' Torquemada threw the crucifix down on a table and left the throne room without another word."

"Oh no!" Mama said. "How did their majesties respond?"

"The queen's face was as white as the wings of a dove. Seneor could only stare, but Abravanel tried to address her. She silenced him with a wave of her hand. 'Do you believe that this comes upon you from the king and me?' she asked them in a terrible voice. 'The Lord has put this thing into our hearts!' Ferdinand touched her arm. 'Let us not be hasty,' he said. 'If Don Isaac offers us thirty thousand gold ducats – ' But the queen interrupted him. 'It is God's will,' she said angrily. 'Go!' she commanded Abravanel and Seneor. 'Go now! You have your answer!'"

Although I wanted to hear more, and I knew that it was unusual for Mama to let me listen in on the two of them talking, the wine was doing its work. "I'm going to bed, Mama, Papa."

"Remember, not a word of any of this to anyone." Papa's warning sounded desperate and forlorn.

CHAPTER 10

SUNDAY, APRIL 29, 1492 –
MONDAY, APRIL 30, 1492

The clanging church bells made my head pound. My stomach churned with fear. I had to warn Yonah somehow. I longed to tell Mama what I wanted to do. I was afraid of her anger, but I knew that she would forgive me eventually and give me good advice. Sofia appeared at my door.

"It's time for mass, mistress."

"I am not going today."

Her eyebrows rose, but she said nothing.

"I don't feel well. My head hurts. I must talk to my lady mother. Have you seen her?"

"She is in the sitting room."

I got up. "Help me dress."

Mama was sitting by the window, at her needlework.

Her kiss on my forehead felt like the wings of a butterfly.

"You are pale, my love. Are you feeling well?"

"I am fine, but I have to talk to you about something important. You will be angry . . ."

Yussuf entered. He bowed and waited patiently until Mama took notice of him.

"My lady, the cook requests your presence in the kitchen immediately."

Mama lifted her eyes to the heavens. "Am I never to have a moment of peace?" She rose from her seat, putting her needlework beside her. "We'll talk later," she said over her shoulder as she followed the Moor out of the room.

I didn't know what to do. I grabbed a peach from a fruit bowl to take to the garden. I carried Anusim's cage to a stone bench and sat down. The scent of the roses and the pomegranates was overwhelming. Anusim burst into a song of unbearable sweetness. The sun warmed my face as I slurped my way through the peach and thought about everything that I had heard last night. I couldn't alter a royal edict, but if I could warn Yonah, at least he and his father could prepare. I didn't dare to wait any longer for Mama's counsel before I spoke to him. It was too late for that. I would have to go to the Juderia myself. If I slipped out of the house while Mama was occupied in the kitchen, I might be able to return before she even realized that I was gone.

I picked up Anusim's cage and hurried to my room. I put it back on the windowsill and rang for Sofia to bring me the boy's clothes I wore to Rabbi Abenbilla's study group.

I sat down on the edge of my bed to wait for her, forcing myself to breathe slowly to calm down. My eyes fell upon the armoire. Something seemed different about it. I could have sworn that the second drawer was half open when I had hidden the kiddush cup in it. With my heart hammering in my throat, I pulled out the drawer. The cup was still there, wrapped in the folds of a petticoat, exactly where I had left it. *I must have closed the drawer without realizing it,* I told myself. Still, I felt uneasy and decided to hide the cup somewhere else. The only other place I could think of was in my jewelry chest. I took the key out of the vase on top of the armoire and unlocked the chest. I put the cup into it and locked it again. Then I put the key back into its hiding place.

The streets were so full of people that nobody paid attention to the Jewish boy who slipped out of our garden. Somebody jostled me and I bumped into the man in front of me. I could tell by his clothing that he was a member of the potters' guild. He stumbled and dropped the clay urn he was carrying. It shattered.

"A pox on you!" he cried. "But what else can I expect from a vile·Jew?" He grabbed hold of my sleeve and spat in my face. "Somebody call the hermandad! The police!"

"Oh no, you don't!" I kicked him in the shin and he let go. I took off at full speed.

"Stop him! Stop him!" he yelled.

I didn't slow down until I turned the corner. I leaned, panting, against a building and wiped my face with my sleeve and tried to catch my breath. The sound of trumpets and drums was loud. Suddenly, I was swept up in a crowd heading toward the Juderia.

It seemed that all of Toledo was in that mob: women with their market baskets on their hips and nobles in rich velvets and hats with tall plumes surrounded me. There were priests and monks in sober vestments and even more sober faces. I could see members of every guild I could think of, from butchers with bloody aprons to bakers covered in flour from head to toe. I could hear the whips of the flagellants. Professional mourners dressed in white, crying and moaning, followed them. And there were Jews, hundreds of them, in their long cloaks with pointed hoods and circular badges, like the one I was wearing. The Jewish men had long beards, and their wives were modestly clad.

Four heralds stood in front of the gates of the Juderia. My heart began to race. Was I too late? There was another drum roll and the bleat of trumpets. One of the heralds stepped forward and announced that he was the bearer of a proclamation from their royal highnesses, Queen Isabel of Castile and King Ferdinand of Aragon. He unrolled a parchment and began to read.

It was as I had feared. I *was* too late. The Edict of Expulsion was being made public. It stated that Jews had to leave our country by the last day of July of the present year of 1492, never to return on pain of death.

They were allowed to sell their businesses and property, but they were not allowed to take gold, silver, and money with them. Christian citizens were forbidden to aid or shelter any Jews on pain of confiscation by the crown of all of their property.

The words fell on the Jews like arrows. The women wailed and tore at their clothes. An old man beat his chest with his fists. He cried, "What will happen to us? What will happen to us? Where shall we go?" Some people wept and others were struck dumb. Among the Christians, there were those who laughed, but there were also many who shook their heads, grim expressions on their faces.

I caught sight of Yonah talking to a man. They were gesturing angrily. I pushed my way toward Yonah, but the crowd swallowed him up before I reached him.

There was nothing for me to do. I set out for home. I would tell my father what I had heard and seen. He would think of a way to help Yonah and his father.

Dozens of noisy, agitated people were milling in front of our villa. I hung back, afraid that they'd see me in my disguise.

At first, I didn't see my parents. When I finally caught sight of them, I saw that they were surrounded by the servants and a dozen of the Inquisition's famil-iars, distinctive in their sinister black clothing. An alguazil, a constable of the Inquisition, was with them. I thought that I saw Luis, but his back was turned toward me so I couldn't be certain. Two of the Inquisition's men were holding Papa's arms behind his back and kicking him. My father tried to fight back, but to no avail.

"Let go of me, you fools!" he roared.

Mama was sobbing. "Let my husband go!"

"Don't you know who you are dealing with? You'll pay dearly for your actions!" Papa cried.

The constable stepped forward. "We know what we're doing, Don Enrique," he said sheepishly.

"I know you, Miguel Santos," Papa said. "The last I saw you, you were serving drinks in a public house. I always thought that you were a sensible man. Why are you behaving so foolishly? Have I not paid enough for your inn's ale?"

Santos's face turned crimson. He would not meet Papa's eyes. "My lot in life has changed," he growled. "I am a servant of the holy Inquisition now. I am following the orders of the Grand Inquisitor, Tomás de Torquemada."

"I've done nothing!" Papa said. "What am I accused of?"

Santos adjusted the sash around his waist. A dagger peeked out of it. "You know that I can't tell you that, Don Enrique. Their excellencies, the Inquisitors, will tell you all you need to know."

With a wave of his hand, Santos ordered his familiars to march off with my father in the direction of the walls of Toledo.

"I'll be back before you know it!" Papa called to Mama over his shoulder.

Mama's response was a tremulous smile. Only the compulsive curling and uncurling of her fingers showed her terror.

———

The servants turned back to their work. I looked around for Luis, but I couldn't see him anywhere. *I must have been mistaken,* I told myself. What would he have been doing here, watching as Papa was taken away?

Nobody was around to see me climb the servants' staircase, two steps at a time. I sat down on the edge of my bed to catch my breath and rang the bell for my slave.

Sofia's eyes were red.

"Where were you, young mistress? They took the master. They banged on the door, bold as anything, while you were gone. May they be cursed!" She slapped her fist into her palm furiously. "How could I ever believe that the Inquisition was right?"

"I saw it happen. I was at the back of the crowd. Where is my lady mother?"

"She took to her bed, poor lady."

I stood up. "Help me, Sofia. Bring me my pink gown."

Mama was lying motionless on her bed, staring at the wall. I opened the shutters to let in some air. She turned her head toward me.

"They took away your father." Her voice was a mere whisper. "Where were you?"

Now wasn't the time to burden her with Yonah's troubles. "I was having a siesta. It's so hot."

She didn't ask why I had heard nothing. "What shall we do?" She reached out and clutched my arm. "They'll burn him alive!"

"No! They have to let him go. He's done nothing."

I sat down on the edge of her bed and pulled her up to me. She put her head on my shoulder. We sat there, not speaking, but each of us praying silently for Papa's safe return.

"This is my punishment for eating pork," she said.

"Don't be silly. God will forgive you. You only did what you had to do."

She let go of my embrace and stood up. "I pray that God will listen to my voice."

Long after the sun had set and the clouds had hidden the moon, there was loud banging on the front gate. Our prayers had been answered. Santos brought Papa back to us – beaten and bloody, but alive.

We rushed to my father and kissed his bruised cheeks. Santos came into the house with him. He stood beside my father silently, passing a knife from one hand to the other hand over and over again.

The servants were jubilant. Sofia fell to her knees, loudly thanking the Lord for Papa's safe return. Yussuf hovered beside Papa, offering him his arm to lean on.

"We must put you to bed, Enrique," Mama said.

"First, I need to do something," Papa replied. "Yussuf, fetch my purse from my chamber."

The Moor returned with the purse and presented it to my father. I saw the glimmer of gold ducats in Papa's palm. He whispered something into Santos's ear and the two men went outside. When he limped back into the house, Papa was alone and his hand was empty. Mama helped him to a chair and sent the servants back to their duties.

"They said that I was a heretic," Papa said. "They accused me of practicing the old religion in secret. I was warned that the two of you are suspect, too. I told the Inquisitors that nothing could be farther from the truth, that there isn't a more devout Christian family than ours. It was difficult to lie . . ." He wiped his brow gently. "God forgive me, I even said that I abhorred the Jews."

Mama handed him a cup of ale. He drank deeply before speaking again.

"It was strange. They seemed to know the customs of our household. It made me wonder if one of the servants might have discovered our secret and betrayed us. We must be more careful even within the walls of our home. I demanded that I be allowed to confront my false accuser, but they refused to tell me who it was.

"Anybody could be an informer, but I can't believe that any of the servants would be so disloyal," Mama said.

"What about Luis?" I asked. "He comes here often. He knows how we live."

"Isabel might be right," Mama said after a moment.

"Nonsense," Papa said. "Have you lost your senses? Why would Luis inform on me? He will be marrying you, Isabel. He has nothing to gain by my arrest."

Mama nodded her head. "You are probably right, Enrique."

"But Papa . . ."

"Don't upset your father." She clasped his hand, kissed it, and held it to her heart. "They must have beaten you."

Papa nodded. "They did. The good Lord gave me the strength to remain silent. I would not confess. Finally, they let me go."

"They might return!"

He sighed. "They often do. Santos promised to warn me before they come for me again. That'll give me time to hide."

"Do you trust him?" Mama asked.

Papa shrugged. "As long as I can pay him. The man likes his gold."

I was too frightened to say anything more. All I could do was hug Papa close.

It must have been past midnight when we crept into the garden. Papa was carrying a small iron chest. It contained the letter Grand Inquisitor Torquemada's grandmother had written to my great-grandmother. Mama led the way, holding a candle. With her hand she tried to shield the flame from prying eyes in the house. I had a shovel under my arm. Papa had told me to take it from the gardener's shed.

Papa stopped beside the orange tree. "This is a good spot to hide the letter," he whispered. "I wanted both of you to see where it is in case I'm not here and you need to dig it up."

"It's too close to the gate," said Mama.

"That's why nobody would suspect that anything was buried here," he replied, taking the shovel from me.

He began to dig. After he had dug a big enough hole, he put the box inside and shoveled earth on top of it. He tamped down the earth with his shovel until it was impossible to see that anything was buried there. He left Mama and me standing there to put the shovel back into the shed.

"Let them come and search us now," he said quietly

when he came back. "They won't find anything."

We went back to the house. I retrieved the kiddush cup and wrapped it in an old petticoat. I lay on my bed, waiting for my parents to fall asleep. When I could bear to wait no longer I tiptoed to Mama's door. It was silent inside. When I passed Papa's chamber, all I heard was his snoring. I left the house as quietly as I could and found the shovel again. I had walked this path at night so many times I didn't need a candle. I began to dig five paces from the hole that my father had made. It took me a long time to dig the hole, for the earth was hard and dry. I became hot and sweaty, but finally my task was done. I was careful to smooth down the earth over the cup, the way I had seen Papa do it. When I was finished, I paused to listen, to feel the sweet spring air. Except for the songs of the crickets, no creature stirred. I made my way back to the house well satisfied with myself.

CHAPTER 11

MONDAY, JUNE 4, 1492 – TUESDAY, JUNE 5, 1492

I hadn't been able to sleep or eat ever since the Inquisition had taken Papa away. I was terrified that Santos and his henchmen would return. And there was nothing I could do to prevent this from happening.

I was also so worried about Yonah. How could I help him? I was helpless. How could I live without seeing him ever again?

One morning, after a particularly sleepless and fretful night, Mama and Papa found me sitting on a bench, weeping in the courtyard.

"Child, what's wrong? Are you frightened for me?" Papa asked as he sat next to me.

I put my arms around him and laid my head against his chest. "I couldn't bear it if anything happened to you."

"I'll do everything I possibly can to keep the Inquisition away from us."

Mama became emotional again. She, too, had not been herself of late. "Oh, Enrique, I am so frightened for you as well. For all of us! I pray to the almighty day and night to keep us safe."

"And for Yonah," I mumbled, "will you pray to God to keep him safe, too?" I was horrified when I realized what I had said – but it was too late to take back the words.

Papa pulled away from our embrace and grasped my shoulders. "What do you mean? Who is Yonah?"

The urge to unburden my heart was too strong, and when I told him, Papa was furious.

"How could you be so foolish?" he bellowed.

I hung my head.

"Papa is right." Mama shook her head slowly.

I couldn't look at either of them. "I am sorry." The words sounded hollow, even to me.

Mama saw my stricken face and patted my back. "Our daughter has grown up."

Papa's face turned so red that I feared that he would suffer an attack of apoplexy. "What nonsense are you speaking, wife? Don't you understand? This boy is a stranger and he holds our lives in his hands. If he betrays us, we will all burn at the stake."

"Yonah would never betray us!"

He continued as if I hadn't spoken. "Then there's the matter of Luis. Have you forgotten?"

I was almost relieved that we were back to that old argument. "I told you that I don't want to marry Luis. The better I know him, the more I loathe him."

My words agitated Papa even more. "You know our reasons for wanting this marriage!" His voice was becoming louder and louder.

"I hate Luis!"

"We know what's best for you!" Papa cried.

Mama touched his arm. "Calm down, Enrique. The servants will hear you. Her expression softened. "Don't be so angry with Isabel. Have you forgotten how we felt when we were young?"

"Foolish woman. Don't be sentimental, Catarina. Isabel must marry Luis."

She spoke quickly to tide his protests. "I know that. Yonah would be a most unsuitable match. A silversmith . . . we want more for you, Isabel."

"Yonah is a good person, Mama."

"I don't doubt that, but you must remember who you are. His being Jewish complicates the situation even more, makes it more difficult."

"Difficult? *Dangerous* is the word you must use. A Jewish man and a Christian woman? Especially a New

Christian! In this day and age, they would be before the Inquisition in an instant." He shook his head sadly. "Besides, the Jews will be gone in a few weeks. At least that'll end this problem."

I couldn't help it. I began to sob. "I'll never see Yonah again! He is a part of my heart, Papa. I trust him completely. I don't know how I'll live without him."

The trembling of my voice revealed my misery. My father sat quietly beside me.

"All right, Isabel," he said. "I won't change my mind. You must do your duty and marry Luis, but I'll see what I can do to help your friend. After all, he is one of us," he muttered under his breath. He stood up. "I know Natan Abenatar by his work. By repute he is said to be a decent man. We must go and see him."

Papa wore a simple homespun cloak. Yussuf was invisible to the townspeople because he was a slave. My fine clothes were covered with a woolen cloak I borrowed from Sofia. In this way, we walked through the teaming streets of Toledo to the Juderia.

Yonah and his father lived in a tidy building across the street from the main square of the Aljama, the Jewish ghetto. The workshop faced the street, and behind it were several simple rooms where Yonah and

his father lived. We found father and son in the courtyard of the house, surrounded by stacked wooden furniture, household goods, and piles and piles of silver
dishes. Yonah was leading two farriers around the yard,
pointing out certain objects to them. When the men
left, he motioned for us to join him.

"Don Enrique, Isabel." He bowed. "What an honor.
Welcome to our home." He glanced at me, his disquiet
written all over his face. "Let me introduce you to my
father."

Master Abenatar was a few steps away, in deep conversation with a man dressed in the uniform of an
alguazil. The constable had his back to us.

"Money is of no use to you, Abenatar," the alguazil
said. "I will trade you a donkey in exchange for your
house and all of its contents. You will need the donkey
to take your belongings out of the country."

"A donkey! The house alone is worth more than
that. And there is all the silver I use for my trade," protested Master Abenatar.

"You can't take your silver or gold with you. You
know that. The holy Inquisition will have you drawn
and quartered if you try to smuggle any of it out. Think
it over carefully before you refuse my offer," said the
alguazil. "It might be the best one you'll receive." He
sounded venomous.

"What a scoundrel," Papa muttered. "Master Abenatar, I will give you two donkeys and an ass for your property," he called out loudly. "Even at that price, I will be getting a bargain!"

Master Abenatar and the alguazil turned toward us. And that was when we recognized the constable. It was Miguel Santos, the innkeeper who had come to our house to arrest Papa on behalf of the Inquisition. Papa stepped back, bumping into me. There was no other sign of the dismay he must have felt upon meeting his jailer.

"Don Enrique!" Santos bowed. "I am glad to see you looking so well."

Papa inclined his head slightly. "Why are you here, Santos? Why are you trying to take advantage of Master Abenatar's misfortune?"

"Are you joking, Don Enrique?" Santos laughed. "I am offering what I consider to be fair trade for the Jew's property, but you changed my mind. I withdraw my offer. This Jew is fortunate that you have so much love for his kind. Jews!" He spat on the ground and was gone before Papa could answer him.

"I hope that your kindness won't cause you problems," Yonah's father said.

"Don't worry about him." Papa extended his hand. "I am Enrique de Cardosa."

Master Abenatar's eyes traveled from my father's face to his hand and back to his face again in amazement before putting his own hand into Papa's palm. "I am Natan Abenatar. I have heard of your healing powers, Don Enrique, how even their majesties depend upon your skill."

"I have been told of the greatness of your artistry, Master Abenatar. We have one of your creations, a little gold songbird in a silver cage. We admire it every day."

"Thank you, Don Enrique," the goldsmith said. "Your offer for my property is most generous. Two donkeys are more than adequate. There is no need to add an ass to the price."

Papa held up his hands. "Indeed there is, Master Abenatar. The price I offered you is fair. I refuse to take advantage of your misfortune. I will have the animals delivered to you."

"Does your papa know about us?" I whispered to Yonah while our fathers were talking.

He shook his head.

"I told my parents everything."

"I guess the honest thing to do is to tell my father, too." He pulled Master Abenatar's sleeve.

"What is it, my son?"

"Papa," he said, "there is something I must say to you."

He recounted the story of our friendship from the time we met on the day of my betrothal to the last time that I had seen him, the day of my birthday.

His father's reaction was familiar. "Have you lost your senses, boy, to put yourself and all those around you in danger?"

Papa tried to calm him down. "Don't judge your son harshly, Master Abenatar. Young people don't think like we do. Our children like each other. It clouded their judgment, made them forget that the Inquisition does not tolerate such a relationship. If any of this would become known, the Inquisition would charge Isabel with heresy immediately. Yonah would be accused of encouraging her to practice the Jewish religion in secret."

"You are right, Don Enrique," said the goldsmith. "We live in terrible times."

"Don Enrique and Isabel are anusim," Yonah said. "They honor our traditions."

"Hush, boy!" his father said. He looked around the yard. "The walls have ears nowadays. Do you want your friends on the stake?"

"I must remind you, Master Abenatar, that Isabel is betrothed to Luis, the son of Alfonso de Carrera," Papa said. "The de Carreras are Old Christians. I am determined that this marriage take place. A marriage with the de Carrera heir will protect my daughter and her foolhardy ways from the Inquisition."

"Please, Papa – " I started.

"Hush, child! You don't know what is best for you."

Yonah did not utter a single word. His silence made me furious.

"Why aren't you standing up for me? Don't you want to be with me?"

His face was pale. "I do want to be with you," he said finally. "It breaks my heart to say it, but your father is right. We can never marry. You know that a Jew and a Christian can never be together. I deluded myself for a while, under the magic of that wretched orange tree. In the cold light of day, I see how wrong I was. We must not see each other again. You have to marry Luis. He will protect you from the Inquisition – and I can't. I will have to leave Sefarad in a few weeks. I can never return."

I grabbed his arm. "I will never see you again!"

He removed my fingers and left the courtyard.

CHAPTER 12

WEDNESDAY, JUNE 20, 1492 – MONDAY, JULY 2, 1492

I was dreaming of Yonah when they came again. Yonah and I floated above an orange grove, holding hands. My little lark was flying ahead of us, leading the way with its beautiful song. My parents and Master Abenatar stood below, smiling and waving. Suddenly, the bird's song died in its throat. The flapping of its wings became frantic – louder and louder.

There was banging in the house. I put on a robe and hurried down the stairs. The soldiers of the Inquisition were dragging my father into the night. I will never forget the gleam of moonlight on cold steel, the dreadful snarl on Santos's face, or the agony in my father's eyes as he tried to resist. I rushed up to Mama to console her. There was nothing to do but hold each other.

Once again, Mama spent her days locked in her chamber, praying.

I sat in my room, my memories my only companions. I couldn't allow myself to think of what was happening to Papa. Instead, I thought of the garden, and of Yonah, and of how much I missed him. I thought about Brianda and her lively chatter. I hadn't seen her for so long.

When I couldn't distract myself any longer, my thoughts returned to Papa. I prayed to the good Lord to keep him safe and to send him home to us. We waited and waited, but this time God did not listen. Seven long days and nights passed and there was still no news of my father. I had to do something. Not knowing was worse than the worst news could possibly be.

Mama was sitting in the rose garden, her needlework lying untouched in her lap. She was so still that a bee buzzing around her mistook her for a flower and landed on her shoulder. I swatted it away.

She looked up, startled. Her voice was flat when she spoke. "We will never see your Papa again," she said. "They'll burn him alive." Each quiet word was a dagger in my heart.

I knelt beside her and lay my hand on hers. "You mustn't say that. We must do something to save him!"

She brushed away my hand. "What can we do?

What can we do? Everybody is afraid of the Inquisition. I am, too. Nobody dares to lift a finger to help us!"

I paused for a moment. I knew what had to be said, but it was still difficult to utter the words. "I'll talk to Luis. Soon, I will be his wife. He'll ask his father to help us. Don Alfonso is powerful. The Inquisition will listen to him. Isn't that why you and Papa want me to marry Luis?"

"I can't ask you to do that," she said, standing up. She began to pace. "I told your father that we made a mistake. You detest the boy, and I don't blame you. He is a graceless brute. I've long suspected that he may have informed on your father to the Inquisition."

"I do, too, Mama. But if he wants to, he could help Papa."

"I don't want you to do that. I forbid you to ask him for help. You were right about him, Isabel. We did a terrible thing in promising you to him. And if he was the one who informed on Papa, we could be in more trouble by asking him for help."

"That doesn't matter now, Mama. If he asks his father, and Don Alonso agrees to intercede with the Inquisition on Papa's behalf, the sacrifice of marrying him is well worth it. We have no choice. We must seek Luis's help if we want to see Papa again."

———

I wrote a note asking Luis to come to see me immediately, and then I rang for Yussuf. The Moor entered the dining hall with his head lowered and his eyes downcast. When he looked up, I saw that his eyes were red, as if he had been weeping.

"Young mistress, I wish that I could do something to help you free Don Enrique. He is the kindest of masters." Tears pooled in his eyes.

I, too, felt like crying, but I told myself firmly that tears would not bring Papa home. I asked Yussuf to deliver the message to Luis's lodgings. "Please tell Don Luis that I must talk to him."

He fell to his knees. "Young mistress, forgive me if I am speaking out of turn, but there is something that I must say to you." He wrung his hands.

"What is it?"

"Please don't hold against me what I am about to tell you."

"Of course I won't." I had to lean forward to hear him.

"Young mistress, be careful when you talk to Don Luis. He is no friend of yours or of your father's."

"Why do you say that, Yussuf?"

"I've seen him drinking with the Inquisition's familiars."

I motioned for him to stand up. "I know what you

are telling me is the truth. You have proven your loyalty to my family over and over again in the past, and you have done so again today."

He struggled to his feet. "I would do anything to help Don Enrique."

"Then you will ask Don Luis to come and see me. I have no choice. I must talk to him. Don't worry. I'll be careful."

He bowed and left the room.

While he was gone, I patted my hair into place and pinched my cheeks to make them rosier. I sat down on a stool so that my blue velvet gown could be seen to full advantage. My hands were clasped together tightly to still their trembling as I plotted what I would say to Luis.

After an hour, Yussuf returned. He announced Luis, who swaggered into the room. I stood up and curtsied deeply.

"My lord . . ." I forced a smile.

"You wanted to see me?" He came closer and towered above me, scowling, his legs wide apart.

I took a deep breath. "I need your help. My papa . . ." I wiped my eyes. "If you would ask your respected father to intercede with the Inquisition on my father's behalf, the Inquisitors might let my papa go."

He stepped even closer and bent toward me.

I steeled myself not to flinch when I tasted his foul breath.

"So, my lady, you aren't so high and mighty now that you need my help?"

I pressed my hand to my breast to still my racing heart. "My lord, I beseech you. Please help my father!"

"Why should I? The holy Inquisition must have good reasons for questioning him."

"My papa is innocent."

"Of course you would say that. I have some advice for you. You should be more careful of the company you keep and the things you hide in your room if you don't want to join your father at the stake."

I pretended that I couldn't hear his mocking tone. I smiled and leaned toward him. "You should help me because we will marry soon," I whispered, placing my fingers on his hand, which rested on his hip. I closed my eyes, waiting for his kiss.

He flicked his fingers against my cheek. "Marry?" he asked. "We'll see about that!"

He turned on his heels and then he was gone.

I was becoming more frightened with each day that passed. I sought out Mama in her room. She was sitting in front of a pier glass. Her maid was brushing her hair while another slave fanned her. She seemed to be in a trance. Her shoulders were slumped and her eyes were closed.

"I must speak to you, Mama."

Slowly, she turned her head. "Yes?"

"Privately."

She dismissed the servants with a motion of her hand. I closed the door, waited a minute, and then opened it again quickly. The corridor was empty.

"We must help Papa before he is tried and it's too late."

"What can we do? I would give my life to free your father." She wiped her eyes.

"There is only one thing left. We must tell Fray Torquemada about the letter you found. If we tell the Grand Inquisitor about the letter, he'll let Papa go. Torquemada doesn't want anybody to know that he is a New Christian."

"Think, girl! I told your father that he was wrong. If we threaten Torquemada, he'll arrest us, too. That won't help." She pulled me so close that I could barely breathe, her arms wrapped around my middle as I stood before her. "I will not put your life in danger," she cried. "Papa wouldn't want me to."

"There is no other way – "

She let go of me and held up her hand. "I don't

want to listen to you. There must be something else we can do." She stood up and began to pace the room. She stopped in front of me. "We must go see Juana. She has always known about our Jewish ancestors, but she has never spoken of them to anyone. She'll help us."

"She won't, Mama. She is a good Catholic. She thinks that we are condemned to hell. That's why she speaks of the Grand Inquisitor with such admiration."

"That doesn't matter! Juana has been a sister to me. Our families have known each other forever. Juana is your godmother. Diego has great influence. She will make sure that he'll help your father."

She sounded so definite that I almost believed her.

She rang the bell and ordered Yussuf to get the litter ready.

"Faster, faster!" Mama called to the slaves carrying us on their shoulders.

They picked up speed as we bounced up and down, up and down, until my teeth chattered. I kept fanning myself, but my clothes were sticking to my body in the summer heat. The hair at the nape of my neck was wet, and I could feel perspiration running down between my shoulder blades. We were traveling so fast that Yussuf, walking behind the litter, had to break into a trot to keep up with us. Before long, we arrived in front of Tia Juana's house.

"My lady, do you want me to ring?" Yussuf asked.

"No! Help me out."

Mama climbed out of the litter and ran up the steps to the heavy oak door. I followed her. We could hear muffled voices and footsteps through the open windows above us. Mama pulled the iron bell. The door did not open. She pounded on the door. It became quiet inside the house.

"Why aren't they opening the door?" she asked. "Where could they be?"

The litter bearers began to whisper among themselves.

I walked down the steps and looked up at the windows. I thought that I saw a movement behind the curtains. "Let's go home, Mama. Tia Juana won't let us in."

"That's not possible." Her face was flushed. She banged on the door with all her might. The house remained silent.

I took her arm. "We're not doing any good by standing here." I pulled her toward the litter.

"There must be some explanation. Juana would never refuse to receive us. We are like sisters," she repeated all the way home. "Where could Juana have gone without telling me?" She wiped her eyes. "I don't understand why the servants didn't answer the door. Something must be wrong." She sighed. "What shall we do?"

"We will have to use great-grandmother's letter."

"And risk torture or worse? It's out of the question."

"We've tried everything else. We have no choice, Mama."

"I'll go to see your father. He'll tell me what to do."

"But how can we get permission to see him?"

"We can't. Not from the Inquisition. But there is always another way. Somebody we can bribe."

She was deep in thought the rest of our journey. When the bearers finally lowered the litter to the ground, Luis and his slave Habib were waiting for us in front of the villa. Habib was holding the reins of two horses and a mule packed with provisions.

Luis greeted us awkwardly. "I came to say good-bye."

Mama pointed to the animals. "What is the meaning of this? Where are you going?"

Luis's face turned crimson. "I received word from my father that he needs me at my home." He mounted one of the horses and with a curt nod galloped off.

His servant set off after him, pulling the mule behind him.

"Good riddance!" Mama said.

I agreed wholeheartedly.

CHAPTER 13

TUESDAY, JULY 3, 1492 –
WEDNESDAY, JULY 4, 1492

Mama and I were panting as we followed Yussuf up the steep hill leading to the alcazar. The palace served both as the headquarters of the Inquisition and as Fray Torquemada's residence when he visited Toledo. Candlelight flickered through the windows on the second floor and we could hear the lilting music of harps and tinkling laughter.

"The Grand Inquisitor must be entertaining tonight," I whispered to Yussuf.

"Lucky for us. The noise made by the friar's guests will cover any noise we might make. It will distract the guards."

We followed the Moor along a lane running next to the stone wall of the palace. It was as dark as pitch. Black clouds obscured the moon's cold light. The ground was uneven, and Mama stumbled. I caught her arm.

"Hold on! We're almost there," Yussuf whispered.

We finally arrived at a wooden gate half-hidden by tall cypress bushes. The Moor knocked on the door three times. It swung open. A disembodied face appeared and floated toward me in the darkness. I clamped my hand over my mouth to stifle a scream.

"Come in," the head said. It floated even closer.

Only then did I see the rest of him – the body of a familiar dressed in black clothes. I saw the exchange of coins Yussuf had asked for before we left.

"Follow me," the man said.

I held on tight to Mama's arm as the familiar led us across the courtyard to a door leading into the alcazar. We followed right behind him as he descended a slippery, worn stone staircase dimly lit by torches on the wall. He stopped in front of a rusty, studded iron door and unlocked it with one of the keys hanging on his belt.

"Five minutes," he said. "That's all you have."

He pushed us through the doorway and then he was gone. The three of us found ourselves in a dark, dank cave full of shadows. A barred window high up on the wall afforded the tiniest bit of light to go by. I almost gagged at the overwhelming stench of blood and excrement. I lifted the hem of my skirt to keep it out of the disgusting, thick sludge that covered the floor. Lying on filthy straw, spectral creatures were chained to the wall. One wild-eyed man dressed in rags, his face streaked with blood, moaned piteously. A pregnant woman, her hands clasped over her swollen belly, lay beside him. I looked away from her nakedness. Many of the prisoners had no clothes. Some were unmoving, silent as ghosts. Others were crying in desperation. A woman held out her arms toward me but did not utter a single word. The clanging of the prisoners' chains echoed off the stone walls.

"Dear God," Mama said, "where is your father?"

Suddenly, a cry. "Catarina! Isabel! Is it you?"

The voice came from a man chained to the wall beneath the window. I examined his grimy features, snowy hair, and scraggly beard. Rags covered his gaunt body. I was sure that I had never seen him before. Mama ran up to him and embraced him.

"Stop, Mama! Have you lost your mind?" I tried to pull her away from him.

"Daughter, don't you know your own father?" he asked.

The voice was Papa's voice. Could it be? I stepped closer. A feeble ray of moonlight lit the man's face. Papa's thick black hair had turned completely white. He had become an old man in just a few weeks, but he was my father. I fell to my knees and kissed his hand. Yussuf kneeled and kissed his feet.

"What have they done to you, my Enrique?" Mama asked.

"Master! May Allah be blessed. We found you alive!" Yussuf said.

"Have you lost your minds to come here?" Papa's voice still held his old authority. "Don't you know what could happen to you?"

"I don't care," Mama said, smoothing his face.

"We want to talk to you," I whispered. "I can't convince Mama that I must speak to the Grand Inquisitor to free you."

"I will not have her put herself in such terrible danger." Mama said.

I crouched as close to Papa as I could because I didn't want the other prisoners to overhear us. "There is nothing else we can do." I told him how Luis rejected my pleas for help. I described the closed doors of Tia Juana's house. "You see? I must go to Torquemada and ask him to release you from prison."

Papa opened his mouth to reply but coughed instead. When he wiped his mouth, I saw blood.

"I'm afraid the danger is probably upon you already. We have nothing to lose. I cannot last much longer here," he said. "God, forgive me, but I agree to your plan, daughter. Go see Torquemada."

"I will go with you, Isabel," Mama said.

"No. I must go by myself. He is more likely to listen to me if there are no witnesses present."

"Then I'll talk to him!" Mama cried. "I don't want you to go. It's too dangerous."

I tried to calm her down. "We can decide later which one of us will see the Grand Inquisitor."

"Don't fool yourselves," Papa said. "Torquemada might arrest you on the spot."

"He won't, Papa. As long as I don't give him his grandmother's letter, he won't harm me. I'll tell him that the letter is hidden in a safe place. I'll be respectful but firm."

"Isabel," Mama said, "I will be the one to see . . ."

Papa tried to stand up, but he sank to his knees. Mama reached for him, but he held up his hand.

"They had me on the rack. My legs . . . it'll take time . . . never mind that now. Tell the Grand Inquisitor how delighted you were to discover that he was a kin and a New Christian like your papa."

"I'll tell him that putting you into prison was a mistake. I'll ask him to set you free."

He squeezed my shoulder. "Do you realize that talking to him may cost you your life? Are you willing to take such a chance?"

I spoke quickly to forestall Mama from interrupting me. "I'll do whatever it takes. I can't bear this. I miss you."

Papa leaned forward and kissed my cheek, then Mama's face. "I have the best wife and daughter in the world. It's not too late to change your minds."

"I don't intend to," Mama said.

"Neither do I," I told him.

I started silently plotting how I could arrange an interview with the Grand Inquisitor without Mama finding out.

Papa's whispered voice was urgent. "All right, but be careful. Tell Torquemada that his refusal to help a relative hurts you deeply. Explain to him that he leaves you no choice but to show the letter to the queen and to the king. Tell him that you are certain that their Catholic majesties hold him in such high regard that they will not allow his kinsman to go to the stake." The words had taken all his energy. His head fell to his chest. "I am tired," he muttered. "I cannot talk anymore."

I grabbed his hands. "Don't lose hope, Papa. I will make sure that the Grand Inquisitor listens. There is nothing he wants less than to have his Converso origins made public."

"Mama, please!"

"You must go before they find you here," Papa said.
We bid him a sad farewell.

"You'll be home before you know it, my dear husband."

Mama's soothing words did nothing to reassure me. I was not sure that Papa had even heard them.

Mama dismissed Yussuf as soon as we came through the front door. When the Moor left, she turned on me.

"How can you imagine that I would allow you to go to the Grand Inquisitor?" she shouted.

"But Mama . . ."

She shook her head. "No more arguments. Not now. I am weary. I must lie down. We'll talk tomorrow," she said as she mounted the stairs.

I waited for a few moments until I was sure that she was in her room. Then I went into the garden, got a shovel from the shed, and headed toward the orange tree. I began to dig. It took me a long time because the packed earth was still dry and hard. I was hot and sweaty by the time the shovel hit the top of the iron chest with a clunk. I lifted out the chest and carefully filled the hole up with the loose dirt. I took the chest back to my room.

I rang for Sofia to bring me a bottle of ink and a quill. I made a faithful copy of the letter. I hid the original letter in my jewelry box and then locked the box. I put it back into my armoire and hid the key in the vase. I hid the empty iron chest under my bed and put the copy of the letter under my pillow. I decided that I would ask Yussuf to take the chest away tomorrow.

Chapter 14

Thursday, July 5, 1492

Iknew Mama was exhausted and would be sleeping soundly. At the first light of dawn, I was able to tiptoe out of the house without waking her. The slaves carried me in the litter to the alcazar and lowered it to the ground. I peeked out through a slit in the drapery. A dozen of the Inquisition's armed guards were stationed in front of the palace. Yussuf, who had followed me on foot, parted the curtains and stuck his head inside.

"What do you want me to do, my lady?"

"Tell the captain of the guards that I seek an audience with his excellency, Tomás de Torquemada." I slipped a few maravedis into his palm. "Sweeten your request with these coins."

The Moor approached the guards. He was too far away for me to hear what he was saying, but I saw one of them point to a man standing apart from the group.

Yussuf bowed before the captain and said something to him. The man shook his head. Yussuf nodded in my direction, and I watched as once again he discreetly paid a bribe.

The Moor came back to the litter smiling.

"It's arranged, young mistress. The power of money never fails. The captain of the guards will escort us inside," he said as he helped me out of the litter.

We followed the captain into the alcazar. I patted my chest through the crimson cloak that covered my dress. With my finger I traced the outline of the copy of my great-grandmother Miriam's letter, which I had pinned to the lining of the cloak. It made me feel a little less afraid. *Both Yonah and I have badges now,* I told myself. *The only difference is that nobody can see mine.*

The guard led us into a large hall with a stone floor. Rich tapestries depicting the twelve apostles and Christ on the cross, wearing a crown of thorns, covered the walls. The hall was unfurnished except for a carved bench. A wooden staircase rose in the center of the room.

"Wait here," the captain said before disappearing through a heavy door set into the wall. We waited and waited, hour after hour, but he did not return. I spent the time rehearsing in my mind what I would say to the Grand Inquisitor, while Yussuf watched on. I was thirsty and my legs were cramping, but I did not care how long I had to wait. The memory of Papa's haunted eyes gave me strength.

"Mistress, perhaps we should go home," Yussuf said.

"Not until I talk to the Grand Inquisitor."

He shook his head but didn't argue.

Finally, the door swung open. A tall, heavy-set Dominican monk came into the hall. The captain was behind him. I curtsied as the monk approached me.

"What are you doing here?" He turned to the captain. "I told you to send them home."

The captain hung his head.

"Father, I must see his excellency, Fray Torquemada," I said. "It's a question of life and death."

"It always is," the monk said in a chilly tone. "You've been waiting all this time?"

"Yes, Father. I beseech you to tell his grace that Doña Isabel de Cardosa, the daughter of Enrique de Cardosa, their majesties' physician, requests an audience with him."

The monk's face grew less frosty and he dismissed the captain with a wave of his hand. "I am Fray Armand of Pensacola. I am his grace's secretary. His grace is not granting audiences today. He is occupied with holy business. Come back another day, Doña Isabel."

I walked over to the bench and sat down. I kept my eyes lowered modestly and fanned myself slowly, as if I had all the time in the world. "I'll wait here until his excellency can find a moment to see me."

The friar stared at me, a puzzled expression on his face. It was obvious that he wasn't used to having his orders questioned. I kept on fanning myself and prayed that he couldn't see or hear the thumping of my heart.

"All right," he finally said. "I'll see what I can do."

He bowed and left the room. Yussuf and I stared at each other, afraid to speak. I remembered Mama's warning that the walls had ears where the Inquisition was concerned.

After what seemed like hours but must have been mere minutes, Fray Armand reappeared.

"You're most fortunate, my child. His grace has granted you an audience. He asked me to tell you that he has but a few minutes to spare."

We followed Fray Armand up the staircase and started down a long corridor lined with doors. A man came out of one of the rooms. His head was turned away and he was moving quickly. I caught a glimpse of his cape as he turned the corner to another hallway. There was something familiar about him. I realized that the way he was moving reminded me of Tio Diego. I opened my mouth to call after him but stopped myself. What would my uncle be doing in the Grand Inquisitor's palace? I dismissed all thoughts of Tio Diego when Fray Armand stopped in front of a door at the very end of the hall. A familiar with a dagger tucked into his black sash was leaning against it. He straightened up at the sight of us and saluted smartly.

"Father Armand! What can I do for you?" he asked.

"Announce Doña Isabel de Cardosa to his excellency."

The familiar swung the door open and I followed him into the chamber. Both Yussuf and the monk stayed behind.

"Doña Isabel de Cardosa to see your grace," the familiar announced. He backed out of the room and gently closed the door.

I waited for the Grand Inquisitor to acknowledge me. A magnificent candelabra obscured my view of Torquemada, sitting behind it, across the room. I had only a glimpse of the top of his head, with its monk's tonsure. Behind this hidden figure stood a familiar. I looked around the room to calm myself. It was a large chamber that was dark even in the daytime. There were no windows. Burning torches cast mysterious shadows.

The walls were whitewashed, matching the snowy damask tablecloth that covered a long, carved table in the middle of the room. It was set with a wealth of silver dishes.

"Hurry up, you fool! I am hungry," cried a petulant voice. I recognized it immediately. The man peered around the candelabra. It was the Grand Inquisitor himself.

"Doña Isabel? Come closer."

My knees were knocking so hard that I could barely cross the long expanse of carpet to his table. I was too frightened to meet his eyes, so I fixed my gaze on a unicorn's horn that lay on the table in front of him. It was the first unicorn's horn that I had ever seen, for they are very rare. Papa had shown me a drawing of one in a book when I was a little girl. He told me that it had magical powers.

A piece of dark bread rested on a silver plate. Beside it was a bowl of dates. A dish of gruel looked so unappetizing that I wouldn't have offered it to one of my servants. The familiar tasted everything on the table.

"The food is safe to eat, your excellency," he said.

The Grand Inquisitor broke off a corner of the bread and chewed it thoughtfully. Suddenly, a small monkey crawled out from underneath the table and hopped up onto the chair next to Torquemada. I was so surprised that I jumped.

"Don't be afraid," Torquemada said. "Miguel is my friend."

Torquemada held out a date. The monkey grabbed it with his paws. Torquemada turned his attention back to me. I curtsied deeply.

"What brings you to my humble lodging, Doña Isabel?"

He did not ask me to sit down, so I remained on my feet, quaking.

"I must speak to you, excellency."

"What can I do for you?"

"I have a delicate matter to discuss, your grace. I would appreciate if my words were heard only by yourself." I nodded my head toward the food taster.

The friar straightened up in his seat. "I believe that we met only once before, Doña Isabel. I barely know your father. How could your words be so important that they must be for my ears only?"

His sharp words stung.

"I am only thinking of you, excellency, not of myself," I muttered. "My request is such that neither you nor I would want to share it with the world."

His eyes narrowed and he waved the food taster out of the room. "You have a lot of gall, my lady. What do you want from me? Be quick. I have but a few moments."

Fear paralyzed me. I tried to speak, but no sound left my throat. Torquemada held out his arm and the monkey hopped onto it. He began to scratch the animal's back.

"What do you want?" he repeated.

"Your excellency, my father . . . my father, Enrique de Cardosa . . ." I finally stammered.

"What about him?"

He began to drum his fingers on top of the table.

I took a deep breath. "Your grace, a terrible injustice has been done. False accusations have been made against my father. The Inquisition arrested him because of them. My father is no heretic. He is a good Christian." All my years of going to Father Juan's mass made this lie easier to tell.

I forced myself to speak in measured tones although I wanted to scream and cry and beat the table with my fists. When the monkey nuzzled Torquemada's chin, the Grand Inquisitor's gaze shifted to his pet. He fed it another date and I began to breathe again.

"How dare you question the holy Inquisition." The cold pebbles that were his eyes bore into my face.

"Your excellency, forgive the love of a daughter for her father." I lowered my voice. "I am certain that you can see that the arrest of one of your own kinsmen must be a mistake. Only a fool would believe that somebody who shares the blood of your excellency would be capable of heresy."

The Grand Inquisitor's hand froze midair for an instant before he resumed feeding his animal. The monkey clapped its paws impatiently.

"What nonsense you speak!" Torquemada said. "Don Enrique is no relative of mine."

"He is, excellency. You must know that your grandmother Sara and my papa's grandmother Miriam were sisters."

His sole reaction to my words was a twitch of his lips.

"I have a letter written by Doña Sara to Doña Miriam. It contains their mother's recipes, recipes for the food your grace's great-grandmother ordered prepared for the Passover." I paused. "That is a Jewish observance, I believe."

Torquemada carefully transferred the date from his palm to the table. The monkey jumped on his shoulder to try and get closer to the date. Roughly, he swept the animal off. The monkey ran to a corner of the room squealing.

"Sit down!" he barked.

I sank down quickly into a chair across from him,

clasped my hands tightly, and crossed my ankles to still their trembling.

"You speak nonsense. Don't you realize that I could have you imprisoned for your lies? You'd never see daylight again." His tone was all the more frightening for its calmness.

"I hope that you wouldn't do that, your grace. I treasure my freedom. That's why I want my papa to be free, too. I must tell you that I left a note to be delivered to their most Catholic majesties if I disappeared or if anything happened to me. I told the queen and the king about my papa's arrest and that my father was made a prisoner through the lies of a cowardly informer. Their majesties will believe me, for I explained that my papa is your cousin. Their majesties hold you in such high regard, excellency, that they would never believe that a kinsman of yours could be a heretic. Unfortunately, the royal couple would also find out that your grace is a New Christian, like my father and me."

"Your allegations are ridiculous! I come from an old Christian family." He was silent for a moment. "Did you bring Doña Sara's letter with you?"

"I was worried that I would lose it, so I put it in a safe place. However, I did copy it for your grace." I handed it to him.

He read it quickly. When he finished, he put the letter down on the table in front of him.

"I want the original of this letter," he said.

"Of course. And you shall have it, excellency, as soon as my father is a free man."

He stared at me for a long moment, as if he wanted to devour my soul. A telltale muscle twitched by his mouth. The only sound in the room came from the rat-a-tat, rat-a-tat of his fingers on the tabletop.

"All right," he finally said. His lips twisted into a wintry smile. "You are quite right, Doña Isabel. Your father seems to be a distant relation of mine. The arrest by the holy Inquisition of one of my kinsmen, regardless how far removed, would be disagreeable to me. I will have Don Enrique freed three days from today."

"Why wait so long?"

"The wait is necessary. I don't want anyone to say that your father was released because you came to see me. You have my word that the Inquisitors will not, shall we say, question him again. I will have Don Enrique taken home. Once he is there, I expect the original of this letter from you."

"You shall have it, your grace," I repeated. I got up from the chair, approached closer, fell to my knees, and kissed his outstretched hand. "Words cannot describe my gratitude."

"No need to thank me. I want justice done."

He stood up and beckoned to his monkey. It crossed the room and jumped into his arms. Torquemada carried it out of the chamber as if it were a baby.

CHAPTER 15

FRIDAY, JULY 6 – SATURDAY, JULY 7, 1492

Mama was pacing the hall when I returned. At first she was furious when I told her that I had gone to the alcazar to speak to the Grand Inquisitor.

"Have you lost your senses? I told you that I would go! Don't you understand the kind of man Torquemada is? Didn't you realize that he could have had you arrested, sent you to the stake? That he still might?" She covered her face with her hands and began to cry. "I couldn't bear losing you, too!"

"You haven't lost me . . . and you haven't lost Papa. Torquemada promised to free him."

I told her everything then – how long Fray Armand kept me waiting, how afraid I had been, how I had persuaded Torquemada to promise to send Papa home.

"At first he paid more attention to his monkey than

to me, but that changed when I told him about Sara's letter to Miriam."

"Do you trust him? Do you believe that he'll let your father go?"

"He will. He doesn't want their majesties to find out that he is a New Christian. Papa will be home three days from today!"

"From your mouth to God's ears!" she said.

The days that followed seemed like an eternity. My mother and I tried to keep each other's spirits up.

We were sitting on a stone bench in the rose garden when Sofia appeared.

"There is somebody at the door to see you, young mistress," she said with an impudent smile.

"Who is it? What are you grinning at?"

She threw a quick glance in my mother's direction and didn't reply.

"What's the matter with you, Sofia? Tell me who is at our door!" I demanded.

"Who is our visitor?" Mama asked.

"Yonah, the silversmith's son."

I got up from the bench but then sat down again. I didn't know what to do. Should I talk to him? He said that we couldn't see each other again. Why did he come?

Mama took the decision out of my hands. "Bring the boy to the garden."

Sofia returned with Yonah in no time and then withdrew. Yonah bowed deeply and then he stood silent, fiddling with his cloak. His color was heightened and he refused to meet my eyes. I forced myself to sit still, with my hands calmly in my lap.

"Doña Catarina, Isabel, my father sends you his greetings," he finally mumbled. "My father and I just heard that Don Enrique was arrested by the Inquisition." His voice became more confident. "What can we do to help?"

"Both you and your father are very kind," Mama said. "But you have enough troubles of your own without involving yourself in ours. We are hopeful that my husband will be a free man very soon." She turned to me. "Isabel, tell Yonah about your interview with the Grand Inquisitor."

Yonah's eyes grew wide as I recounted my tale and told him that Torquemada, Papa, and I shared the same blood. I told him what I had earlier told Mama – that Torquemada wouldn't want the king and queen to discover his Jewish background.

Yonah shook his head. "Somehow it all seems too easy. Why would Torquemada give in so easily? He must have some tricks up his sleeve."

"He may be the cruelest of the cruel, but he is a man of God. Surely, someone in his position must be a man of his word," Mama replied.

Yonah still looked unconvinced.

"If he keeps his side of our bargain, I will give him the letter. I keep my promises."

"I pray that Isabel is right," Mama said. She stood up. "I must go to the kitchen to consult the cook about dinner."

I rose to go with her. A small smile quivered over her lips.

"You stay. The two of you must have a lot to say to each other."

With a wave of her hand, she was gone. I was astonished. What had happened to my proper mother, always so strict about conventions?

"Doña Catarina is a kind lady. I am grateful that she gave me the opportunity to tell you what fills my heart."

I remembered my tears, the sleepless nights, and all the dreams and hopes I had bid farewell to. I realized that Yonah was trying to protect me, but I felt that he gave up on our dreams too easily. I turned my face away.

"There is nothing to talk about," I said. "You told me that you couldn't see me again. That I should marry Luis."

He took my hand. I tried to pull it away, but he wouldn't let it go.

"Don't you understand? I wanted to save us heartbreak, and I was right. In a week's time, my father and I will leave Sefarad, never to return. We will be going to Cartagena, and from there we will sail to Morocco to start new lives. That is my destiny. Yours is to stay here with your parents and marry Luis and become the mistress of a great estate. I came to say good-bye. We'll probably never see each other again."

A lone tear trickled down his cheek. It melted my heart.

"I am here now," I whispered.

Then he kissed me.

CHAPTER 16

SUNDAY, JULY 8, 1492 –
WEDNESDAY, JULY 11, 1492

The sun was rising and the sky was turning a blushing rose when the loud clang of the bell woke me.

I met Mama on the landing. Like me, she was barefoot and covered by a robe.

She dug her fingers into my arm. "Could it be your father? Has he come home?"

We rushed to the front hall. The servants were waiting for us. None of them made the slightest move toward the door.

"Open the door, Yussuf!" Mama cried.

The Moor's fingers fumbled with the locks. Finally, he swung the door open.

Papa fell into Yussuf's arms. Mama and I rushed forward and hugged Papa and kissed him until he asked us to stop.

"Doña Isabel, the Grand Inquisitor instructed me to ask you for a letter you had promised him," said a quiet voice.

I turned around and looked toward the open door. Fray Armand was patiently waiting on the stoop. There was a litter with closed curtains behind him outside.

"Yes, I did promise to give the letter to his grace. I must go to my chamber for it."

He nodded and I left.

It took mere minutes to retrieve the letter from the jewelry chest. I returned to the front hall and handed it to the monk. "This is the letter his excellency is expecting."

I watched him through the open door as he took it to the litter.

"I have it, your grace," I heard him say.

Torquemada's blunt features appeared for a moment in the window of the litter as he reached for the letter through the curtains.

Papa slammed our door shut. "I don't want to see them ever again. It's so good to be home!"

We bathed my father's wounds and put him to bed. He was feverish, so Mama sent for the surgeon to apply leeches to bleed him to balance his humors. We fed him gruel by a spoon and gave him ale to drink to help him recover his strength. Two days later, he was strong enough to leave his bed.

"Master, Yonah Abenatar, the son of the silversmith Natan Abenatar, wishes to speak to you," announced Yussuf.

Papa's eyes flickered in my direction. "Show him in."

The Moor ushered Yonah into the room. Then he bowed and withdrew, closing the door gently behind him.

"Don Enrique, Doña Catarina, Isabel, good afternoon to you all. Forgive me for disturbing you, but I had to speak to you as soon as possible," Yonah said.

Papa asked him to sit down. "What brings you to our home?"

Yonah's eyes traveled around the sitting room. "Can we be overheard?"

Papa shook his head.

"I have some bad news, Don Enrique," he said. "I told Isabel that the Grand Inquisitor gave in to her demands too easily." He lowered his voice. "Unfortunately, my suspicions were well-founded. Pablo, the brother of my father's apprentice, is a footman in Torquemada's household. I asked my father's apprentice to speak to Pablo to find out if he had heard any mention of you, Don Enrique, in the Grand Inquisitor's household."

Papa shifted in his seat. "Has he?"

"I am afraid that he has. Pablo was cleaning silver in the Grand Inquisitor's apartment when Torquemada walked into the chamber, accompanied by Fray Armand. They took no notice of Pablo. They were talking about you, Don Enrique."

"Are you certain that it was of me that they spoke?"

"There is no doubt of that. The Grand Inquisitor referred to you as Enrique de Cardosa of Toledo. He also called you – forgive me for repeating this – Enrique the Jew."

"No offense taken." He gave a rueful laugh. "Torquemada might have been speaking of himself. Our ancestors are the same. What did the Grand Inquisitor say about me?"

Yonah lowered his voice even more. "Torquemada said, and I am quoting him, 'Enrique the Jew believes that he is safe now. I shall let a few days pass to give him time to celebrate his freedom. How dare he send his whelp to blackmail me?'"

Yonah paused, then continued. "Pablo said that the Grand Inquisitor was so angry that he was shouting. This was the first time that Pablo had ever heard him raise his voice."

"What did Torquemada say next?"

"I am sorry to tell you this, Don Enrique, but the Grand Inquisitor plans to arrest not only you but also Doña Catarina and Isabel."

Mama gasped. I started to speak, but Papa silenced me with a wave of his hand.

"We must leave this place as soon as possible," Papa said. "The Inquisition has long arms. Nowhere in Sefarad is safe for us."

"But where can we go?" Mama asked.

"When I told my father what Pablo had said, he came to the same conclusion as you did, Don Enrique – that it is no longer safe for you to remain in the kingdom. He instructed me to invite you and your family to join us when we leave our home in a week's time."

My selfish heart began to dance.

"Where will you go, Yonah?" Papa asked.

"I wanted to sign on as a crew for Christopher Columbus," Yonah answered. "Many people say that he is an anusim. I know several men who are sailing with Columbus. He doesn't ask too many questions when he signs you on." He sighed. "My father says that he is too old to sail with Columbus, and I won't go without him. We'll make our way on foot to Cartagena instead, and board a ship from there to Morocco. My mother, may she rest in peace, had a cousin in Fez. We'll try to find him when we get there."

"Morocco! So far away," Mama said.

Papa rubbed his eyes tiredly. "What do you think, Catarina? Should we accept Natan Abenatar's most generous invitation and go to Morocco with him and Yonah?"

"Morocco is as good a place as any," Mama said. "But must we leave, Enrique? This is our home. This is where you were born. This is all we know." Defeated, she wiped her eyes.

"We are no different from Yonah or his father," Papa said. "They, too, have to leave all that's familiar and beloved. If we stay, we will lose everything, even our lives."

I jumped to my feet. For the first time since I could remember, I laughed. "Thank God! I won't have to marry Luis!"

I stole a look at Yonah. He stared ahead. I couldn't tell how he felt.

"Yonah," Papa said, "please tell your father that we accept his kind offer with gratitude."

Yonah stood up. "I'll convey your message to him, Don Enrique. There is another problem. Where will you hide for the next few days? My father and I can't give you refuge before we leave. The spies of the Inquisition are everywhere in the Juderia."

"We will find a place," Papa said.

"Let us know where you are," Yonah replied. "We will come for you four days from today, early, before the sun rises. I will bring clothing so that you will look like one of us."

Before I knew it, Yonah was at the door.

"I was afraid that this would happen," Papa said after Yonah had left.

"What a fine boy," Mama said. "It's so kind of his father to risk their own safety to help us. It's good to know there are people like that in the world."

"Where will we go to hide?" I asked.

"Juana and Diego will take us in," replied Mama.

"You can't believe that. Tia Juana wouldn't even answer the door when we tried to see her!"

"I can't explain why that happened," Mama said, "but I know Juana. She would never let me down. She is your godmother. She is my friend. She'll help us."

Papa pulled the bell so hard and pounded so fiercely on the front door of Tia Juana's house that I thought that the wood would splinter. However, the door remained closed.

"I told you that we shouldn't have come back. I knew that they wouldn't let us in."

"Silence, Isabel." He banged even harder.

Mama shot me an imploring glance. "Isabel! Don't vex your father. Enrique," she continued, "Isabel is right. Let's go home. Juana and her family may have gone to their orchard to escape the heat." She wiped the sweat off her forehead.

"With all the windows open? Not likely. They are at home but not answering the door," Papa roared. He slapped his thigh in frustration. "We're wasting our time here." He turned to Yussuf, who was holding our horses. "Give me the reins!"

Papa mounted his horse. Mama and I followed on our animals. The Moor rode a donkey. It was slow going with horses, donkeys, mules, litters, and people milling in the road. We had turned the corner when I heard somebody calling after me.

"Isabel, wait!"

Brianda was running through the crowd behind us, pushing and shoving aside everyone in her path with her elbows.

"Stop, Papa! Stop!"

My parents reigned in their horses. Brianda was gasping for breath. I dismounted and hugged her. Mama got off her horse, too, but my father stayed in his saddle.

"Where are your parents?" he thundered. "Why won't they answer the door?"

"I am sorry, Tio Enrique, but – "

"But what?"

"Leave the girl alone, Enrique!" Mama said. Her tone was sharp. "*She* is here, isn't she?"

Papa dismounted. "Your Tia Catarina is right. Forgive my bad manners, Brianda. We need your parents' help, but there is no need to burden you with our problems."

"What's wrong?" Brianda asked.

"The Inquisition came for Papa and . . ."

"Silence, Isabel!" Papa yelled.

"Why can't I tell Brianda about your arrest? Everybody knows about it."

"There is no harm in Brianda knowing," Mama said to Papa. "She will realize how important it is that we find her parents."

"This is not the place to talk," Papa said.

He led us through an alley to a lane behind the shops. It was quieter than the main thoroughfare. He stopped in front of an inn with a thatched roof. We tied our horses to a hitching post in front of it.

"Yussuf, stay with the animals," Papa said. "Don't take your eyes off them, not even for a moment. There are plenty of horse thieves about."

We went into the inn. We found ourselves in a low-ceilinged room with clay walls covered by soot.

We sat on benches beside a rough-hewn table. The proprietor, a surly man with a dirty doublet and even dirtier fingernails, brought us ale. I couldn't bear to touch the tankard he slammed down on the table in front of me.

I told Brianda about everything – about Papa's arrest, about my interview with the Grand Inquisitor, about Torquemada's treachery. She was horrified.

"We have to find a hiding place . . ." I couldn't find the words to say anything more.

Mama said them for me. "If the Grand Inquisitor finds us, he will arrest us. So we must disappear. Where are your parents, my dear? As you can see, we must speak to them. We have little time."

Brianda hung her head. "They're home," she admitted. "My mother told my father not to open the door when you called. You know how he always does what she tells him . . . it's easier. Mother says that you are New Christians – heretics! She says that the Inquisition will punish us if we are your friends, that it is forbidden to help you."

"Are you scared, Brianda? To be my friend?"

"Of course not!" she cried. "How can I help you?"

Mama was wringing her hands. "I would never have believed that Juana was so disloyal."

I knew what was coming next.

Softly, as if to herself, Mama said, "We grew up together, close as sisters."

"Don't judge her harshly," Papa said. "Fear does strange things to people."

"My mother is afraid of the Inquisition," Brianda muttered under her breath.

Mama looked unconvinced. "When times are this hard, you quickly discover who your friends are."

"What can I do for you?" Brianda asked.

Papa threw a few coins on the table and stood up. "Unless you are able to hide a whole family for a few days, there is nothing much you can do for us."

"Wait a minute, Tio Enrique!" Brianda cried. "I have the solution."

Brianda began to drum her fingers on the table, deep in thought. I had the feeling that she had even forgotten that we were with her. Papa sat down again.

"Yes," Brianda said, "I can help you."

"How?" I asked.

She leaned closer. "There is an old shed in the back of our garden. It's overgrown with weeds. Nobody ever goes in there. It's dirty and uncomfortable, but you will be safe there. Nobody will think of looking for you in it. My parents will never know that you are there."

"Do you realize, child, the danger you will be putting yourself in? The Inquisition is merciless. If it ever found out that you helped us . . . well, you know what that would mean."

"Your aunt is right," Papa said. "Think over carefully whether you want to help us. We won't think any less of you if you decide against it."

"I love the mother church, but I must help you. You are my friends," said Brianda firmly. "Come to our house tomorrow, after the moon rises to the top of the sky. The garden wall has a rear gate. Only the servants use it. It opens into the alley behind the house. Somebody will be waiting for you there."

"If we can hide in that shed until we can leave for Morocco, we have a chance of surviving," Papa said as we were nearing the front of our villa. "I just hope that Brianda's courage won't desert her."

"Never! Not in a million years. Brianda has been my best friend forever. I know her better than anyone. She is brave as a lion. She is also loyal and generous." Suddenly, I remembered her treatment of the slave Mara. "Her only fault is that she is sometimes careless of the feelings of others. We can trust her completely, though."

"I am pleased that – "

"Enrique, look!" Mama interrupted. Three horsemen were approaching. "Who are they?"

The horsemen's mounts were kicking up so much dust that it was impossible to identify the men. We waited for them. As the dust settled, Luis and his father appeared before us. Habib, their slave, had accompanied them.

"What is the meaning of this? Why are they here?" Mama whispered. Papa helped her down from her horse.

"I can guess," Papa said, lifting me to the ground. "Let me do the talking, Isabel," he said under his breath.

Don Alfonso, Luis, and the slave dismounted. Luis's father swept his hat off and bowed deeply. Luis merely nodded.

"Don Alfonso, Luis, welcome," Papa said.

"It's nice to see you, Don Enrique." The cavalier bowed to Mama and smiled at me.

Luis handed his reins to his slave. His hat stayed on top of his head.

"You are just in time to share a meal with us," Mama said.

Don Alfonso shifted from one foot to the other. "We don't want to put you to any trouble, Doña Catarina. However, I would like to have a word with your husband."

Luis fixed his gaze on the ground and remained silent.

Papa led us into the dining hall.

"At least you must have some ale," Mama said.

"I won't say no, mistress. Traveling during the summer is thirsty business."

We settled around the table. Don Alfonso seemed nervous, fingering his mustache. Luis stared into the air, as if he didn't see any of us.

A servant brought tankards of ale and set them down on the table. Don Alfonso drank greedily, but Luis pushed his cup away as if the mere sight of it made him sick.

Finally, Don Alfonso put his tankard down. "Don Enrique, Doña Catarina, Doña Isabel, you must be wondering why we are here."

"You are always most welcome in our home," Papa said pleasantly.

Don Alfonso began to fidget with the handle of his sword. When he finally raised his head, I was struck by the sadness in his eyes. "What I have to tell you is most distasteful to me as a cavalier. We live in perilous times. The Inquisition – "

"Father! Have you lost your mind?" Luis cried. He jumped up and thumped the table. "What my father is trying to tell you is that I refuse to marry the whelp of a heretic!"

My father rose in his seat, his hand on the dagger

tucked into the sash at his waist. "How dare you talk to us like this!" He glared at Luis.

"I dare more than you know, Don Enrique," Luis said. "Haven't you learned your lesson yet? Don't you understand that the Inquisition has long arms? I would be more careful if I were in your shoes."

Papa took a step forward and drew his dagger.

Mama plucked at his sleeve. "Enrique! You are forgetting yourself!" she cried. "Don Alfonso and his son are guests in our home."

"Have you lost your wits, boy, to use such a tone?" Don Alfonso took Luis by the shoulders and shook him hard. "Be silent if you know what's good for you!"

Luis sat down and turned his head away, but not before I saw the twist of his lips. Papa took a deep breath and sat down. Don Alfonso began to speak again.

"Don Enrique, Doña Catarina, it breaks my heart to tell you that a match between your daughter and my son cannot take place now." He turned toward me. "I am sorry, Isabel, but such a union is no longer practical, or even safe, in the wicked times in which we find ourselves." He gulped down more of his ale. "I hope that I have your agreement to the dissolution of the betrothal contract between our children," he said to my parents. "And of course the dowry . . . I have spent some of the portion I already received."

I felt Luis's eyes on me, full of contempt. I didn't care. I wanted to cry from happiness. I was no longer betrothed! I was free in the eyes of the law. I wondered what Yonah would say. I lowered my head so that my face wouldn't betray me.

My parents exchanged quick glances.

"You have my agreement, Don Alfonso, to the breaking of the betrothal contract," Papa said. "Return to me as much of the dowry as you can. The rest can be given back later."

"I have long thought that our children would not be happy together," Mama added.

Don Alfonso bent his head. "You are both kinder than I deserve. If we lived in another time . . . if the Inquisition wouldn't have . . ." His voice broke.

Luis took a long drink from his tankard. "At last I have something to celebrate."

"I would never have believed that Alfonso de Carrera would break his word," Papa said after Luis and his father left.

Mama shrugged her shoulders. "Isabel would have been miserable living with that creature."

"It's over and done with now," Papa said. "You were right. Luis must have reported me to the Inquisition."

"He probably did, but we'll never know for sure," Mama said. "Thank God that Isabel doesn't have to marry him."

"I couldn't be happier about it," I said as I kissed their cheeks.

Mama stood up. "Let's go upstairs. We can't take much with us tomorrow night. I want to sort through my clothes."

I went up to my chamber. It was hard to believe that I would be spending only one more night within the four walls that had been my home for as long as I could remember. I opened the shutters and the window. Dappled sunlight snaked into the room. I wandered around, touching my belongings. I picked up an earthenware cup full of smooth stones Brianda and I had collected when we were young girls. I folded a shawl I had carelessly thrown down on my bed. I took my jewelry chest out of the armoire and unlocked it. I tried on the necklace Brianda had given me for the last time. I put it back into the chest with a heavy heart for I knew that the Inquisition forbade Jews from taking gold and silver out of the country. I locked the chest and returned it to the armoire. Finally, I went back to the window. Anusim's cage stood on the windowsill.

The little bird ruffled its feathers when it saw me. I opened the cage door and cradled it in my palm. I smoothed down its feathers with a finger and kissed its head gently. I knew what I had to do. I leaned out of the window and opened my hand. The bird fluttered its wings, and then it was gone. It soared high into the sky before landing on the bough of a tree under the window. It broke into such a sweet song that my heart filled with hope. Then it flew away.

That night, after everyone in the house had gone to sleep, I returned to the orange tree. I dug up the silver kiddush cup Yonah had given me. I hid it among the clothes I had packed in a bundle made out of a petticoat even though I knew I shouldn't. *I will decide what to do with it later on,* I said to myself. I would be taking the bundle with me. I also put into it the boy's clothes that I had worn when I went to the Juderia.

The moonlight crept into the shed through a small window. I could see that somebody had recently tried to clean up the cramped space. The clay floor had been swept clean. Several hoes, rakes, a scythe, and two buckets were piled up in a corner. Three burlap sacks had been laid on the floor as our beds. An unlit tallow candle was placed on a wooden box, a flint beside it.

"I am sorry that I can't make you more comfortable, but I was afraid that somebody would notice if

I had furniture brought in here," Brianda said.

"We'll manage," Mama said.

"We won't be here long. If everything goes according to plan, we'll be gone tomorrow night," Papa added.

"From your mouth to God's ears," Mama and I said together.

"Don't light the candle unless you absolutely have to. I am worried that someone in the house might notice the flame." Brianda walked to the door. "I must go now, before I am missed. My slave will bring you something to eat. I am afraid that it won't be much. My mother knows the contents of our larder to the last mouthful. I don't want her to suspect anything."

"We want to thank you again, Brianda," Mama said. "You are saving our lives at great risk to your own."

Brianda walked back toward us. "I wish that I could do more, Tia Catarina." She wrapped her arms around Mama's waist and put her head on her shoulder. "I just wish that my parents would . . ." Her voice trailed off.

My mother patted her back. "When somebody is afraid, it's hard to do the right thing."

"You have a forgiving soul, Tia Catarina." Brianda straightened up. "I don't dare stay here any longer. Your food will be arriving soon. I told Mara to knock three times when she comes. Don't open the door unless you hear three knocks."

"Can you trust the slave?" Mama asked.

"Absolutely!"

"You said that she was stupid and clumsy," I said.

"You know this slave girl?" Mama asked me.

"You've seen her, too, Mama, the last time we visited Tia Juana. She served us cakes."

"Ah yes. The girl with the ebony face."

Brianda had the grace to blush. "You know my cursed temper. Mother is always telling me to control myself. After you left that day, I told Mara that I realized that it wasn't her fault that the cake fell to the floor. She is reliable – the only one among the servants who wouldn't betray us," she said as she walked back to the door and left us. The door clicked shut behind her.

As soon as she was gone, I realized that we had forgotten to say good-bye. I wanted to run after her, but Papa grabbed my arm.

"Do you want us caught? Let her go!"

"But I'll never see her again!"

"That can't be helped."

I knew that he was right, but it still hurt. I buried my face in Mama's neck. When I was finally able to stop my tears, I settled down on one of the burlap sacks.

Mara brought us dark bread, a chunk of cheese, and some ale for our supper. After we finished eating, we sat in the darkness for a while, talking. I couldn't stop thinking of Anusim, and of the sweet song I'd never hear again. I also remembered all the fun Brianda and I had together.

"We might as well try to get some sleep," Papa said. "I'll go to Natan Abenatar's house tomorrow morning and let him know where we are."

"No, Papa! It's too dangerous for you to go. The Grand Inquisitor's men will spot you right away. I'll go."

"Absolutely not! I – "

Mama stopped him. "Isabel can do it – she'll have many dangers to face. This isn't the greatest of them."

Papa grudgingly agreed, and before long I heard him snoring on his scrap of burlap. I lay in the darkness, my palms sweaty. I traced the outline of the kiddush cup in my bundle and felt better. I began to pray. I prayed that Torquemada's cruelty would not affect us again. I prayed that all would go well tomorrow night and that we would be able to leave our beloved Sefarad with Yonah and his father. I also prayed that Yonah and I would . . . I wasn't sure how to complete this prayer. I fell asleep and Anusim serenaded me in my dreams.

CHAPTER 17

THURSDAY, JULY 12, 1492

The Juderia was a place of ghosts. The streets were completely deserted. Gone were the merchants selling their wares. There was no sign of women gossiping in the doorways. The children playing in the streets had vanished. The horses, the donkeys, and the carts that the animals pulled had disappeared. And strangest of all was the silence. The noise of the throngs who frequented the lanes and alleys of the Juderia was stilled.

I began to worry. Had everybody gone already? Had we been left behind? I told myself not to be foolish. Yonah would never leave without saying good-bye and telling us of the change in his plans.

The silversmith's shop was deserted. I banged on the front door, but nobody opened it. I was about to leave when I heard a faint, distant sound.

I followed it to the yard behind the house. A youth, stripped to the waist under the hot July sun, was breaking a wooden table into pieces with an ax.

"What are you doing?"

He whipped around. He was a boy about my own age with dark hair. The metal cross at his throat gleamed in the sunlight. He held his ax pressed against his bare chest, as if it were a weapon. "Who are you? What do you want? There is nothing left here for you if you are one of them scavengers!"

"I am not!" I answered.

His grip on the handle of his ax tightened.

"I am Yaacov, Yonah's friend. Where can I find him?" I struck out my hand.

He looked suspicious but finally grasped it. "Your hand is soft, like a woman's," he muttered.

"Where can I find Yonah?"

His eyes traveled warily to the red and white badge on my cloak. "If you are one of them, why don't you know?"

"Know what?"

He wiped his brow with the back of his arm. "All the Jews know."

"I have to tell you the truth. My father is a physician in their majesties' court. He received special dispensation from the queen and the king to live outside the Juderia. I usually meet Yonah in the streets of Toledo. I am not privy to everything that goes on in the Aljama."

"'Dispensation,' 'privy,'" he muttered. "You use big words like the gentry. So do my master and Yonah. You better not be wanting to hurt my master or his son!" he said fiercely.

I realized then that he was the apprentice whose brother Pablo had overheard Torquemada and Fray Armand talking about my papa.

"There is nothing I want to do less than hurt Yonah or Master Abenatar. I told you – Yonah is my friend."

"He better be. There is no master who is kinder or more fair than Master Abenatar. You'd never know that he was a Jew!"

I opened my mouth to ask him what the Jews had done to him to deserve such a hateful remark, but I thought better of it. It was no use making him angry if I wanted him to give me information. "Yonah talked about you to me. He said that you are a loyal person. Where is he? Where is your master? I have to speak to them right away!"

His forehead puckered as he considered my question.

I tried again. "So, what do you say? I have to find Yonah. Where is he?"

"I guess there is no harm in telling you. The Jews have gone to their cemetery."

"Where is it?"

"You really don't know much, do you?"

"I told you why. I don't live in the Juderia."

He pointed to the north. "Follow the lane behind the house to the edge of the Juderia. You can't miss it."

I heard the cries even before I saw the cemetery. It seemed that every Jew in Toledo had gone there to say a last good-bye to their loved ones. I passed graves where bearded men were placing stones on their parents' graves. An old lady sat on the ground beside her long-departed husband's grave, tears streaming down her face. Everywhere, men stood in groups of ten to chant the Mourners' Kaddish in memory of the loved ones they had lost many years ago. The rabbi's wife was hugging a slender, weeping girl.

I looked around but I couldn't see Yonah in the crowd.

"Isabel, is that you?" He had found me. He took my hand. "What are you doing here?"

"I came to tell you that we are hiding in a shed in the garden behind the house of my friend Brianda de Alvarez."

"Brianda de Alvarez? Is she not the daughter of Diego de Alvarez?"

I nodded.

"Diego de Alvarez is a familiar of the Inquisition. He doesn't wear the black clothing of a familiar, like most of them do, but he is one of their informers. I am certain of this."

It took me a moment to understand his words. Tio Diego – an informer? An enemy of our family? Why, he used to carry me on his shoulders when I was a child. We shared meals in each other's homes. He was family. His wife was my godmother, and his daughter my best friend. I remembered for a moment the figure I had seen in the corridor in the Grand Inquisitor's palace. Could that have been Tio Diego? I no longer knew what to think.

"The world doesn't make sense anymore."

Yonah sighed. "No, it certainly doesn't. But I don't understand . . . why would Don Diego want to help you?"

"He doesn't. Neither does his wife. They wouldn't even open their door to us when we went to ask them for help. Tio Diego and Tia Juana don't know that Brianda offered us their shed as a hiding place."

"You're lucky to have such a good friend!"

"I know!" Then, more quietly, I added, "I wanted to tell you something else. Don Alfonso and Luis came to see us. They broke the betrothal contract. I am free."

Yonah grinned. "I am so glad! I must speak to your father."

"Not yet. Not until we are safe again. There is too much on his mind."

He leaned closer. "It won't be easy to wait."

I felt too shy to meet his eyes.

He laughed and released my hand. "Let's go to my papa," he said.

He led me toward a grave a few steps away. Master Abenatar was standing next to it, his back to us. He was rubbing the top of the headstone with a cloth. We were too far away for me to read the inscription on it.

"It's my mother's grave," Yonah said. "My baby brother is buried beside her. Papa," he said, "look!"

Natan Abenatar turned around. He stared at me for a long moment before holding out his hand. "Doña Isabel, I almost didn't recognize you in these clothes. Are you all right?"

"I am, because of you. I came to thank you for offering us a way to freedom."

The pious man did not want to hear my words. "It is I who should be thanking you, Doña Isabel. I am grateful that I can offer help to your family. The Talmud says that if you save one life, you save the world." He rubbed the headstone again. "Who would have thought . . ." He shook his head. "We will come for you at sunrise." His eyes roamed around the cemetery. "It is so hard to leave our loved ones. We haven't the power to withstand the injustices heaped upon our heads."

"What do you mean, Papa?"

"I heard that Rabbi Seneor was baptized, as was his whole family."

"Oh, Papa, no."

"Don't judge him too harshly, son. Seneor is an old man. Rumor has it that he agreed to his baptism in order to save the lives of our people."

"What about Isaac Abravanel?" Yonah asked.

"They tried to force the baptism font upon him by attempting to kidnap his grandson, but Abravanel beat them at their own game. Abravanel is still a Jew and will die a Jew."

Abravanel and Seneor – why were these names so familiar to me? I thought to myself. Then I recalled what I had heard about them. They were the Jewish courtiers who had tried to prevent the expulsion of the Jews from the kingdom. Abravanel even offered the queen and the king thirty thousand gold ducats of his own money if they let the Jews remain in Sefarad. I remembered how Papa had admired their courage.

Tears filled Master Abenatar's eyes. "Yonah and I came to the cemetery to say good-bye to my beloved

Tova and my little Simon." He drew a finger along the rough edge of the headstone. "I pray that the good Lord guides us to safety and to new lives, just as he led our people out of Egypt."

CHAPTER 18

FRIDAY, JULY 13, 1492

The shed was stifling and airless in the summer heat. It was hard to know if morning had come because a thick mist blanketed the garden. I had perched myself at the small shed window, to watch for any strangers, when I saw the shape of a man. He came closer and stopped in the doorway. I could finally see his face. It was Yonah. He was carrying a parcel in his hand.

"I have a surprise for you," he announced after greeting us.

He stepped aside and motioned behind him with his hand. Out of the shadows came Yussuf and Sofia. Both slaves were dressed like Yonah. They came inside and I closed the door behind them.

"What are you doing here?" Mama whispered urgently.

Sofia dropped to her knees. She grabbed Mama's hand and kissed it. "Forgive me for coming, my lady, but I could not bear being separated from my young mistress."

Mama pulled her up from the ground. "Don't be foolish. Don't you realize what could happen to you if you stay with us? The Inquisition might capture you. You might go hungry. Return home! It's not too late. Nobody knows yet that you came to us."

Sofia hung her head. I put my arm around her shoulders.

Mama turned to Yussuf. Gently, she said, "I am disappointed in you. You should have known better."

The Moor bowed deeply. "Forgive me, Doña Catarina. Let us come with you. We'll be of use to you."

I couldn't remain silent any longer. "Please let them stay, Mama. I would miss them more than I can say."

"You are being selfish, Isabel. If the Grand Inquisitor's people capture us, what do you think will happen to Sofia and Yussuf? They are slaves."

"They won't catch us. I am sure of it." I prayed quickly that I was right. "With us gone, Sofia and Yussuf would get a new master. Who knows how he would treat them? He might be cruel to them."

"Isabel is right," Papa said. "Yussuf and Sofia are

here already, so let them stay for now. We'll part from them in Cartagena."

Mama nodded, but I could see that she wasn't happy with Papa's decision.

"Let's not worry about what'll happen in Cartagena until we get there," I said.

"Thank you, master, mistress," Yussuf said, bowing again. "You won't regret your decision."

Sofia was beaming from ear to ear.

"How did you find us?" Papa asked.

Sofia glanced at me. "I was certain that Master Yonah would know where my young mistress was. Yussuf and I went to the Juderia to find him. Fortune was on our side. Master Yonah was just leaving his home to come to you when we arrived."

"Sofia is more clever than the familiars or the alguazil," Yussuf said. "They couldn't find you, Don Enrique, but she did. Santos led Torquemada's men when they came for you last night. Santos is so full of hate. They tore the house apart looking for you."

"They threatened Yussuf with torture if he didn't tell them where you were," Sofia said. "They punched him in the stomach many times." She shook her head. "And to think that only a few months ago I thought that the Inquisition was fair and just!"

"Are you all right, Yussuf?" Mama cried.

"I am fine, my lady. I told them over and over again that I didn't know how to find you. They finally left. Santos promised that they would be back. I believe him. I give thanks to Allah that you got away."

Mama began to cross herself, but then she let her hand drop. "Old habits die hard. I, too, thank the Lord for saving our lives."

"After Santos and the familiars were gone, Yussuf and I decided to find you and to warn you."

Yussuf looked at Yonah and shook his head. "It took a lot of convincing for Master Yonah to agree to us coming with him." He smiled. "He is even more strong-minded than you, Don Enrique."

"But not more stubborn than you," Yonah laughed.

The rising sun was burning away the mist.

"We must leave before we are discovered," Papa said.

Yonah handed the package he was cradling to my mother. "These are the clothes we have to wear. It'll be safer for you to look like one of us."

"We *are* one of you," Papa said.

We waited outside while my parents changed into their new clothes. Don Enrique de Cardosa and his lady wife were transformed into a Jewish couple with red and white badges on the shoulders of their cloaks. Next it was my turn. I put on the boy's clothes I had worn to the Juderia. Suddenly, I thought of the silver kiddush cup Yonah had given me. I knew that I was forbidden to take it with me because we were pretending to be Jews, but I couldn't bear to part with it. The petticoat I had taken off was lying in a heap on the clay floor. I tore a long strip of lace from the hem and tied it tightly around the cup. Then I wound the lace around my waist, so that the cup hung from my waist.

We followed Yonah through the sleeping streets. I tried to memorize everything that I saw. Here was Butchers' Lane, where we always bought our meat. We passed the Church of Santo Tome, where Alberto had swung his sambenito high up into the air.

At the edge of town, we came upon an incredible sight. A long, long line of people was trudging down the dirt road as far as the eye could see. We began to walk along the column of people, in search of Yonah's father. I saw courtiers and scholars and silversmiths like Natan Abenatar. There were farmers and innkeepers. Most people walked on foot along the rutted path. The swollen-bellied pregnant women and infirm were in carts pulled by donkeys.

Rabbis encouraged the people to sing hymns.

I saw an old man fall to the ground. Despite his friends' pleas, he could not get up. They had to leave him behind. Farther down the road, the crowd parted to walk around a girl bent over the body of a woman.

"Mama, don't die! Don't die!" she wailed.

A newborn baby's tiny cries came from the back of a donkey cart. *One dead, one born,* I thought.

Even though it was early in the morning, the air shimmered in the heat. But the heat did not stop priests and monks in long cassocks, who held crosses high, from running along the line of people.

"Repent! Repent! Give yourself up to Christ!" they exhorted the marchers.

Most of the exiles ignored them, but there were those who bent their knees to the cross to be baptized.

We walked around a group of flagellants.

"Repent! Repent!" they chanted.

I was careful not to look at their bloodied bodies, but I could not shut out the sound of whips meeting flesh.

"Where could my father be?" Yonah asked, scanning the faces of the people who walked by. "Ah! There he is." Yonah pointed to our left.

"I was getting worried," Master Abenatar said when we approached.

"Everything is fine. No one saw us leave," Yonah said.

"We are grateful to you," Papa said.

Yonah's father inclined his head. "You and your family are a part of us now, Don Enrique."

"We most certainly are," Papa said.

"Is that you, Isabel?" a voice called out.

Rabbi Abenbilla and Yehudit came up to us. I introduced them to my parents.

"I am so happy that you are here!" Yehudit cried as we embraced each other.

"We are honored that you are coming with us," the rabbi said.

Yehudit led me over to a group of girls dancing close to us. They were holding hands while they bowed and dipped and kicked, all the while moving at the same pace as the line of people surrounding them.

Before I knew it, the world became a kaleidoscope of color and laughter.

The line of people came to a sudden stop. I stumbled, lost my balance, and fell on the uneven ground, scraping my knee. As I struggled to get up, I lifted my head and locked eyes with Brianda's father, my Tio Diego. He was mounted on a black stallion. Beside him was Santos on a white mare. They were surrounded by a dozen familiars on horseback. Daggers hung from their waists.

"What are you doing?" Santos shouted at me. "Why are you on the ground?"

Tio Diego's eyes flickered in recognition as he met my gaze. He did not say a single word.

"I tripped, my lord," I muttered, "the ground is uneven."

I saw Papa take a step toward me, but Natan Abenatar pulled him back. Papa bent his head as if to examine the bundle at his feet. My mother turned her head away, pretending to speak to a neighbor. Sofia and Yussuf leaned toward each other, whispering.

Santos's eyes traveled through the crowd. "Those wretched Marranos might be hiding anywhere," he yelled, jumping off his horse. "We must look closer."

"Don't waste your time, Santos. It's obvious that they aren't here," Tio Diego said. "Let us return to the alcazar and tell his grace that we didn't find Don Enrique and his family with the Jews. They must have made their way to a port and are hiding on one of the galleons."

"You are right, Don Diego," Santos said, mounting his horse. "Let's go!"

He whipped his horse and galloped off. Tio Diego did not look back. I began to breathe again.

CHAPTER 19

SATURDAY, JULY 14, 1492 –
MONDAY, JULY 16, 1492

The dancing and music stopped as the day turned into night and night turned to day again. We walked with our belongings heavy on our backs. Our numbers became fewer as we split into groups. Most of the Jews of Sefarad headed toward the Extremadura Mountains. They had to cross the tall peaks to reach Portugal. Other refugees headed to the seaports of Tortosa, Tarragona, Barcelona, and Valencia. Groups sailed from Cadiz and Malaga. Some turned north to Navarre or sailed far away from Laredo on the Cantabrian coast. We were on our way to the seaport of Cartagena, where ships were waiting to transport the Jews of Spain to their new homes. We wanted to try our fortunes in Morocco.

The heat was relentless. We rose early to begin our

journey, rested in the middle of the day when the sun was overhead, and began to walk again after the sun started its descent in the sky. For the last two days, we hadn't been able to find water. There was no brook or lake where we could fill our jugs. My mouth was constantly dry and full of dirt from the dust the hot winds blew about on the arid plain. I tried to keep my mind blank. I did not want to remember the soft bed I used to sleep in, the savory tidbits of food our cook prepared for me, the cool ale we drank at the dinner table, or the scented baths Sofia prepared in the old metal tub in my chamber.

We had walked for three days when I began to feel that I could not take another step. I just wanted to lie down on the scrubby path – but I dared not. There were vultures circling above us, and I knew that they would swoop down on a prone body. Yesterday, when a woman fainted, they swarmed her immediately. Her son had to beat them off with a stick to save her from an unspeakable death. I knew that I had to go on and, with all the will I had, I forced myself to put one foot in front of the other.

Master Abenatar and Yonah were walking in front of me. They led three mules packed high. Two were the animals Papa had given them as payment for their house. My parents, their faces covered in grime, looked like strangers. My talkative mother did not utter a word of complaint. Whenever Sofia and Yussuf offered to carry the bundle she had slung over her shoulder, she refused.

"Carry your own burden. It's heavy enough," she said.

Papa offered her his arm, but she was determined to walk on her own.

I tapped Yonah on the shoulder. "I have to rest. I am tired and thirsty and all I want to do is sleep."

He looked into the sky at the vultures. "I wouldn't advise it. Stay strong. We must be more than halfway to Cartagena."

As we approached the top of the hill, I heard the sound of gurgling water. I hastened my steps and there it was! Below us lay an oasis of green – a bubbling brook shaded by olive trees. "I must pinch myself. Am I dreaming?"

"If you are, we are dreaming together," Yonah said excitedly.

"Thank you, Lord of the universe, for your mercy!" cried Master Abenatar.

Papa led the way. He grabbed my hand, I took Mama's, and we rushed down the hill. The others followed our lead. We were tired, dirty, and joyous. I bent my head to the babbling stream and drank deeply. I rinsed away the dirt from my face, my hands, and even my hair.

The men broke branches off an olive tree and sharpened the tips of the branches with their knives. The stream was teeming with fish. The men had no problem spearing the fish with their sharp sticks. We gathered a mountain of twigs, lit them, and roasted the fish over the open fire. We finished the delicious meal with wild pears plucked off the trees and figs we had brought with us from home.

"We'll rest under the trees until the sun sets," Papa said. He turned to me. "Isabel, I need a piece of white cloth. Did you bring anything like that with you?

"I have handkerchiefs. What do you want to do with them?"

He laughed. "You ask too many questions. Can you spare two of your handkerchiefs?"

I opened my bundle and found them for him.

"Just what I needed." He broke a small twig off an olive tree and whittled it down until its tip was very fine. Next, he held the tip of the stick over the fire until it glowed bright. When it had cooled to form charcoal, he sat down under one of the trees and used the twig to write on each of the handkerchiefs.

The sunshine and my full stomach made my eyes heavy. I used the bundle I was carrying as a pillow and lay down on the grass. I wondered what Papa was writing, but I was too tired to ask. I was so exhausted that I fell into a deep, restless sleep. I dreamed of Anusim, singing his song of freedom, of Brianda, so brave and loyal, and of the Grand Inquisitor, his face contorted with anger when he realized that we had escaped his clutches.

I awoke suddenly to someone pulling my arm. The sun was beginning to set, and Yonah was bent over me.

"Leave me alone! Let me sleep."

"Quiet!" He pressed his hand to my mouth.

I saw two horsemen at the edge of our little camp. They were hard-faced brigands in grimy clothes and even grimier faces. Curved swords hung at their waists and they held daggers in their hands.

"Oh, dear God! Bandits!" Yehudit cried.

"Give us your gold!" thundered one of the thieves.

We remained silent.

"Are you all deaf?"

"We don't have gold," my father said in an even voice. "We have nothing to give you. We are Jews who were forced to leave our homes in Toledo in the Kingdom of Castile. We were not allowed to take anything of value with us."

"Jews always have gold!" snarled the bandit. He climbed down from his horse and grabbed Yehudit's neck, pulling her close and holding his dagger against her throat. Yehudit's mother cried out. Yehudit's face became wet with tears and sweat.

"Hand over your gold, Jew, or the wench is dead!" the brigand yelled.

"I told you. We have nothing of value," Papa said. He threw his bundle at the brigand's feet. "Here, take what little food we have left."

"Please, sir – let my daughter go!" Yehudit's father begged.

The brigand opened my father's bundle and kicked it away. Dry meat and figs rolled in all directions. Two vultures descended and began to peck at it.

"Give me your gold!" the bandit yelled again.

I remembered the kiddush cup tied to my waist. I turned away, reached under my clothes, and tore the cup off the strip of lace that held it in place.

"You there!" the bandit shouted. "What are you doing?"

I held the cup out toward him. It shone in the sun's fading rays. "Here, sir," I said. "The cup is for you. It's made of silver. It's worth a lot of money."

He grabbed it out of my hand and turned it over. He spat on it. "It's got Jew writing on it. I don't want it."

"We have nothing else to give you. The cup is made of silver. It's valuable."

"Why do you care if it's Jew stuff?" the second brigand asked. "We can trade it for something else."

The bandit pushed Yehudit away so roughly that she fell to the ground. He wiped the cup clean with his sleeve and shoved it under his clothing. Then he climbed back on his horse and without another word the pair galloped off.

Yonah picked up a stick and chased away the feasting birds. He carefully gathered up what was left of the food and packed it back into Papa's bundle. "We'll need every bit," he said.

"You are a brave girl, Isabel!" Yehudit's mother cried.

Yehudit embraced me, but Papa was angry.

"You silly girl," he shouted. "You took a big chance bringing a silver cup with you. Do you realize what would have happened to you if the Inquisition's men found it on you?"

"But they didn't, Enrique," Mama said. "Isabel saved Yehudit's life. They might have killed that child – or worse!" She shuddered.

"She *did* save her life," Papa said grudgingly. He picked up his load. "We must start walking again."

"I am so frightened," Yehudit complained. "I can't go on."

"The brigands might return. Do you want to

chance it?" I held out my arm.

Yehudit took it. Her weight was heavy against my shoulder.

"Don't despair, my children," said Rabbi Abenbilla. "The Lord led us out of Egypt. He parted the Red Sea for our people's safe passage. He will do the same for us in Cartagena."

"I hope that you are right, Rabbi," I said. "We can't go on like this much longer."

CHAPTER 20

FRIDAY, JULY 20, 1492 –
SUNDAY, JULY 22, 1492

O n the morning of the third day after the robbery, we joined hundreds of people streaming from all directions toward the sea. I saw a man carrying his little son on his shoulders while his wife supported her aged mother. Ten children followed their father and pregnant mother, the older ones carrying the young ones in their arms. Everybody was excited, even the sick and the infirm. For the first time in what seemed like an eternity, I heard laughter.

A man called out, "The almighty will save us!"

Someone else shouted, "He will part the sea and lead us to freedom just as he led our ancestors out of Egypt!"

"He will lead us to freedom! He will lead us to freedom!" the crowd began to chant.

A smudge of dark blue appeared on the horizon. Mama cried out. "The ocean!"

"Our future," Yonah whispered to me.

We picked up our pace and soon we were in Cartagena. We passed the humble dwellings lining the streets of the town and finally arrived at the port. Six galleons were dancing on the blue sea.

Somewhere in the crowd a man began to sing "Dayenu."

"It's a song we sing at Passover," explained Yonah, his eyes filling with tears.

A woman's voice joined in, then another voice began to sing, and another after him until a thousand throats expressed their gratitude to God:

"If He had given us their wealth,
and had not split the sea for us
– Dayenu, it would have sufficed!

If He had split the sea for us,
and had not taken us through it on dry land
– Dayenu, it would have sufficed!

If He had taken us through the sea on dry land,
and had not drowned our oppressors in it
– Dayenu, it would have sufficed!

If he had drowned our oppressors in it,
and had not supplied our needs in the desert for forty years
– Dayenu, it would have sufficed!"

Finally, the song ended and the noise subsided. We waited and waited and waited for a miracle to occur. Nothing happened. The waves did not part and the ocean remained calm. The flags of the ships fluttered gently.

Instead, priests carrying crosses appeared.

"Repent! Repent!" they cried. "Accept Christ and you will be saved!"

For a moment, I was back in church in my usual pew, with Father Juan conducting mass. I heard the music; I smelled the incense; I tasted the host. The familiarity of it all tugged at my heart. I thought of the heavenly peace I felt when I prayed to the blessed Virgin. I felt like me when I thought these things. I looked at Yonah. Would I ever become the person he wanted me to be? I didn't know.

"We must go to the ships or we won't get a berth," Yonah said.

"You're right," Papa added. He looked around. "There are so many of us."

"The almighty will help us," said Master Abenatar.

"I wish that I had your faith," Papa said.

Sofia nudged me with her elbow. "Mistress," she said, "I have something of yours that might be useful. Before we left, I went to your room to look for the necklace that Doña Brianda had given you, but I couldn't find it anywhere."

"It's in my jewelry chest."

"I thought that it might be but I didn't dare to bring the jewelry chest with me. It's too big. But I did bring this!"

She took a garish gold bracelet out of the bundle over her shoulder, the bracelet that Luis had given me for my birthday. She held it up. "It was thrown down on a table in your room. I know that you don't like it, young mistress, but it must be valuable. I heard that you were forbidden to take gold with you, but nobody would suspect somebody like me of having such a bracelet." She handed it to Papa. "Don Enrique, will it help you arrange a passage for us on one of the ships?"

Papa's eyes gleamed. "It'll get a berth for all of us – for our family and for Yonah and his father, for Rabbi Abenbilla and his family, and for Yehudit and her parents."

He led the way as we pushed through hundreds of people waiting at the harbor, holding onto one another's clothing to keep together. At the edge of the ocean, we passed a large group kneeling on the ground while a priest was pouring holy water over their heads to baptize them. Papa stopped.

"Sofia, Yussuf, we must bid you farewell here."

From the bundle slung over his shoulder, he drew out the two white handkerchiefs on which he had written. He handed the first handkerchief to Yussuf, the second to Sofia.

"What is this, master?" the Moor asked.

"A document that grants you your freedom. The charcoal is a little smeared, but the words are clear enough to prove that you are no longer slaves. Both of you are free!"

Tears came to Yussuf's eyes. "May Allah bless you, master! I will never forget your kindness. It's hard to leave you."

"Where will you go?" Papa asked.

"I will roam the kingdom until I find my wife and child. I heard that they were in Aragon." He bowed deeply for the last time and melted away into the crowd.

"I thank you, Don Enrique, from the bottom of my heart," Sofia said. She knelt at my feet. "Let me stay with you, Doña Isabel. *You* are my family!"

I glanced at Mama, and she nodded her head. I pulled Sofia close.

"Only if you come with us as my sister, not as my servant," I told her as we clasped hands.

Papa led us up the gangplank of the *Santa Maria*. We were fortunate. The ship was about to sail and we were the last passengers allowed to board. We pressed against the ship's railing while Papa negotiated our passage with the captain. Yonah's shoulder was warm against mine. Yehudit and my mother stood on my other side. The sailors hoisted up the gangplank and unfurled the sails. My eyes drank in the contours of the shoreline, the green trees, the hazy mountains in the distance, and the houses dotting the landscape of my beloved Sefarad.

The ship began its journey and the land began to recede until I could no longer see even a glimpse of it. I wiped away my tears and put my head on Yonah's shoulder. He took my hand. We stared into the horizon together.

Lowell School
1640 Kalmia Road, NW
Washington, DC 20012